Tulips in the Sand

A Riley Matthews Mystery

By: Caryn Gottlieb FitzGerald

Cover art: Spotlight Marketing and Design

Printed in the United States of America

Caryn Gottlieb-FitzGerald, Publisher

P.O. Box 1343

Mansfield, TX 76063

Library of Congress Cataloging-in-Publication Data

Gottlieb FitzGerald, Caryn

Tulips in the Sand ~ A Riley Matthews Mystery

ISBN: 978-0-6152-1500-6

Tulips in the Sand

"Ok, here you go, Mrs. Murphy, just sign on the bottom and you'll be all set."

She smiled without thinking. A big grin that must have taken the sales girl by surprise because she asked, "Mrs. Murphy, is everything okay?"

"Oh, yes," realizing her actions seemed odd, she added, "everything is just perfect."

With that, she signed the charge receipt, took her package, mumbled a thank you and left the store. Once outside, the sun warmed her face, and her smile returned. She remembered the simple comment the sales girl had made which caused her to smile so happily. The simple action of calling her "Mrs. Murphy", that was it, just hearing those words referring to her, was enough to cause her to be overcome with happiness and smile beyond control. As she continued down the tree lined street, she thought back to a time many years ago when becoming "Mrs. Murphy" seemed like a dream that would never come true.

Chapter One - Ten years earlier

It was Kim's idea to go to the Squeaky Hinge Bar and Grill. Riley had thought about it for a moment and was not too keen on the idea.

"Oh, Riley, come on! We'll go, listen to some music, have a drink or two and be home early. It's not a big deal, and it'll be fun."

"Okay Kim, we'll go, but you're driving."

"See you then, be ready" Riley said as she hung up the phone, chuckling to herself. For some reason the comment, "be ready" coming from Kim was amusing, since Kim was almost never on time. It was a standing joke that whatever time Kim said to be ready, figure fifteen more minutes before she would arrive. Looking at the clock Riley realized she had plenty of time to take a nap before tonight's outing. She set her alarm for 7 o'clock and dozed off.

Surprisingly enough, Kim was on time, eight thirty on the dot the doorbell rang. The girls did a last minute hair and makeup check and out the door they went.

The Squeaky Hinge was more than twenty minutes away, but Kim was sure it would be fun and worth the drive, so Riley agreed. Kim had found the place through some friends and figured it would do Riley some good to go someplace other than the normal local hangouts. Riley had been dating a local bartender, Tony and although he was nice enough, she was not sure if he was "the one" for her, he had his mood swings and was not always pleasant to be around. However she found by dating him no one asked her for ID when she went to a local bar and being twenty in a state where the legal drinking age is twenty-one, this was an added benefit. When Riley had asked Kim about getting in to the bar without ID, Kim said her friend Kelly knew the house band and had introduced her, so therefore they could walk in with them, no questions asked.

The Squeaky Hinge was a restaurant with a large bar area. It sat in the middle of a strip mall with a dozen or so other stores and restaurants, nothing special.

Their timing was impeccable, as they drove into the parking lot; Kim honked her horn at a guy unloading his truck. "Hey Danny!" she yelled out the window, "how's it going?"

Riley looked at the man, he appeared to be in his late twenties or early thirties. He had a stocky build with brown hair. Riley was not sure as to what he was unloading from his truck, but they looked like large black boxes. Kim parked two spots over and as they got out of the car, Danny was headed towards them.

"Hey Kim, what's up?" He leaned over to kiss her, it appeared he was going for the lips, but Kim was too quick and he got her cheek instead. He laughed, as though he was used to getting "the cheek" and then realized that there was another person standing with Kim. "Who's your friend?"

Riley felt as though she was a piece of meat being checked out by a butcher. Danny was giving her the once over and she was not too thrilled with the inspection.

"This is my friend Riley."

Danny smiled and leaned over to kiss Riley, again aiming for the lips. Riley, however, was aware of where he was going and turned her cheek to him; once again, Danny got "the cheek".

"Nice to meet you," he said. "Are you from here?"

Riley replied simply, not wanting to engage in conversation with this guy who seemed to enjoy talking to her chest. "Originally, up north, but I've been here a couple of years."

Danny seemed satisfied with her answer. Either that or he was distracted by the time, because he asked no more questions. He turned back to his truck, grabbed another of the big black boxes, which Riley now realized were speakers and headed towards the back door.

"Come on, you two, grab something and follow me," he said as he walked away.

"Here," said Kim and handed Riley a duffel bag, "Come on!" She called behind her as she raced toward the open back door.

Once inside, Riley glanced around. "Not too bad, Kim, kind of family-ish in the day, party-ish at night type of place."

"See, I told you you'd like it."

"Ask me again in an hour, when your friend Danny stops ogling me."

"Don't flatter yourself; he does that to anything female. Good thing you're not wearing a skirt or he'd be all over you like bees on honey."

Riley was suddenly grateful she had chosen her jeans and sweater over the mini-skirt she had almost worn. "So, what kind of music does this band play?"

"Mostly older stuff, but every now and then they throw something new in. You'll like it." Just then the hostess approached and asked, "how many?"

Kim answered her and within a moment she was off. They followed her to a booth near the stage. They sat down, smiled at the waiter and ordered a couple of drinks. While they waited for their drinks Riley noticed that Danny was the only one setting up on stage; everyone else had apparently set up and left the stage.

The smoky environment made Riley lose track of time, soon the band was playing and the dance floor was full. It seemed like only a few moments later when Danny announced the band was taking a break.

"Ok, Kim, I'll admit they are good."

"I knew you'd like them. Believe it or not, they all have other jobs; the band thing is just a weekend gig. Come on, I'll introduce you to everyone else."

"Let's skip that for now, I want to run to the ladies room. I'll be back in a minute." Riley got up and headed toward the flashing neon signs indicating men and women's rooms.

As she headed back to the table, Riley could see the band had already converged upon Kim and she seemed to be enjoying the attention. Riley decided to grab some fresh air before going back to sit with her. She spotted the front door and headed for it.

Outside the front door was a park bench, Riley was about to sit down when she heard a voice, "be careful, that bench is wet."

Riley turned in the direction of the voice and that's when she saw him. He was tall, over six feet, with black hair, blue eyes and a very sexy voice.

"Um, thanks," was all she managed to say.

"Quite welcome," was his reply. "I'm Taylor. And you are?" He extended his hand to shake hers.

"Riley Matthews." Her hand met his; she could not believe the intense feeling in her stomach at that very moment. She was at a loss for words.

"Riley. Pretty name for a pretty lady."

"Thanks," she heard herself utter as she leaned against the building for support. He was incredible. No one had ever called her a pretty lady before; in fact she had always considered herself to be quite plain. She had dark brown hair and eyes, was a medium size four build and just over five foot six. Nothing special to look at, or so she had thought. Until tonight.

"Listen Riley, I've got to get back inside, but it's been nice talking with you, maybe we can do it again sometime."

"Yeah, sure, anytime," she said.

He turned and walked back into the restaurant. In an instant he was gone, she was alone and the night air turned from cool to cold in just a brief moment. A chill ran through her spine and she turned to go back into the building.

"Riley, where were you?" Kim asked. "I was worried when you didn't come back."

"Sorry Kim. I took the long way to the john." She sat down as the lights dimmed, signaling the band was about the start again.

As they sat and chatted, the band played behind them. One song blended into the next, Riley wasn't listening very closely and she doubted Kim was either as they were engrossed in conversation, leaning into each other over the table trying to hear over the music. Until the voice spoke again. Riley was in mid sentence when she heard her name over the microphone. She turned and saw Taylor on stage, 'where did he come from?' she thought as she looked at the stage, 'was he up there before and I just didn't notice him? What is he saying?' She listened more intently and heard him say his next song was for his brown-eyed girl, Riley.

She felt a blush come over her face as she glanced up and found Kim looking at her, asking "how do you know him?"

"I met him when I went outside during the break. I really didn't think anything of it though," she lied. She really had thought a lot of it. There was something about him that made her stomach do flip-flops. He was special. They finished the song, sang a few more and announced they were ending for the night.

Riley looked at her watch, it was after one in the morning! They paid the bill, Kim said she was going to the ladies room and would be right back. Riley began to walk towards the back door, Danny was standing next to Taylor and she figured this was a good opportunity to say goodbye. She walked over. The two men turned and smiled at her.

"How did you like our music?" Danny asked.

"You guys sounded really good. Do you play every weekend?" Riley asked.

"Usually we do, occasionally Taylor's wife throws a fit about him being out so late and then we have to skip a weekend to make her happy." Danny chuckled and walked away, leaving Taylor looking embarrassed.

"Oh, you're married." It wasn't even a question, more of a disappointed remark and Riley didn't even know why she said it out loud, but she did.

"Couple of years. Her name is Jeni. I've also got a little girl, she's two and her name is Kelsey."

"That's nice," she replied as she looked for Kim to come back. All Riley wanted to do at that moment was crawl into a hole, especially since she looked at his hand and there was the ring, big as life, how did she miss it? Just then Kim rounded the corner and Riley felt relieved.

"I'd better go, it's late and we have a long drive. Bye," she said as she raced out the door towards Kim.

"Kim!" she shouted, "Let's go."

Kim looked up, surprised. "Is everything ok?"

"Yeah, I'm just tired," she said as they walked to the car.

"Ok, it's open," Kim said as she unlocked the car doors.

Kim started the engine and waved to Danny as they drove out of the parking lot. Riley closed her eyes and never noticed Taylor standing at the back door, watching them leave.

Chapter 2

Saturday morning the sun flooded Riley's bedroom with light. She glanced at the clock, it's red light flashing six thirty, she had a few more minutes to sleep before she had to get up for work. She closed her eyes and rolled over, but the ring of the phone prevented any further sleep. She answered the phone knowing who it would be without even hearing a voice on the other end.

"Morning Tony," she mumbled into the phone.

"Hey, where were you last night? I tried to call you until midnight, nobody answered. What's up?"

"I went out with Kim, we saw a late movie." She didn't know why she was lying to him. She hadn't done anything wrong, and besides that he was half drunk. In five hours he wouldn't even remember talking to her.

"Oh, well, I wanted you to come into the bar and meet some of my old high school buddies. We even went out to some late night clubs after I got done at three; I wanted you to be there."

Riley thought, as clearly as she could when functioning on only a few hours sleep, "let me guess, you're just getting home now, right?"

"You got it hon, want to come over and tuck me in?"

"Tony, I've got to be at work in less than an hour. Call me when you get up this afternoon, ok?" Silence. When dealing with a normal person, Riley would have been concerned that there was no response to her question. When dealing with Tony, however, Riley knew what to expect.

"Tony?" she waited. No reply. She covered her left ear and listened into the phone with her right. There it was, the faint sound of Tony snoring. He was asleep, no need to worry. She rolled over and hung up the phone. Glancing at the clock, she realized that she no longer had time for an extra few minutes of sleep, so she pushed back the covers and headed for the bathroom.

The day was halfway sunny, nothing too different from any other March day in Florida. She headed to the doctors office where she had worked since her junior year in high school. The only bad thing about working there is the Saturday morning thing, she would have much rather slept in like most of her friends, but then again, she didn't have to work late nights like most of them, so it balanced out.

The morning went by quickly; patients in, patients out, nothing out of the ordinary. Riley found herself thinking about Taylor, she was curious about him. She realized that aside from his name, she really knew nothing else about him. The one thing she did know was he was married with a child, not good. On the one hand, Riley was telling herself to forget about him immediately, but something inside her was saying "there is something here".

The office closed at two, and Riley figured Tony had enough time to sleep, so she headed for his house to wake him up. She knocked on the door, no answer.

"Darn," she said to herself as she fumbled through her pockets for the key. She found it and opened the door. "Tony?" she called, "you up?"

No response.

Dropping her bag on the table, Riley headed upstairs, still calling his name. From the bedroom, she heard the sound of the fan. Figuring he was still sleeping, she slowly opened the door. The bedroom was a mess, clothes from the previous night thrown on the floor, forming an obstacle course. She stepped around them, into the room.

"Tony?" she said hesitantly, "where are you?"

At that moment, someone grabbed her from behind, scooped her up and tossed her on the bed. In an instant he was on top of her, kissing her neck, running his hands through her hair.

"Tony, are you crazy! You scared me half to death."

"You are so sexy, you drive me wild!"

She had to smile. Even with all his faults, he was a good guy most of the time. They spent the next few hours in bed, doing the one thing she had no complaints about with him, having sex.

Four o'clock rolled around quickly and the alarm rang through the room, waking Tony for his evening shift at the bar. He obviously heard the alarm before she did as she heard his voice, "Riley, wake up."

She looked at him, not realizing she had fallen asleep.

"What time is it?" She asked groggily.

"Almost four, I've got to get to work, do you have your key?"

"Yeah, it's here somewhere."

"Good, lock up when you leave. Unless, you'd like to stay permanently?" She knew where he was going with this comment; he had asked her to move in with him several times, she kept putting him off.

"Tony, I am not even going to discuss this with you now, you have to get to work."

"At least come up to the bar later and visit me."

"I'll be there. Now get out of here, before you're late and that boss of yours decides to fire you."

He leaned over and kissed her goodbye. "Later." He closed the door and she heard him going down the stairs.

"Later, Taylor." She whispered under her breath as she rolled over and went back to sleep.

It was after seven when she awoke. At first she rolled over to reach for Tony and then realizing he was at work, pulled her hand back. She stretched and got out of bed. It was useless to look for her clothes in the mess on the floor, so she pulled a fresh pair of shorts and a T-shirt out of the closet, dressed quickly and went downstairs. Finding nothing to eat in the fridge, she grabbed her bag and headed out the door into the crisp evening air.

Once in the car, she found her hunger was more intense than before. "Probably because you haven't eaten since this morning silly," she said out loud surprising herself. She turned into the drive-thru and ordered a combo meal to eat on the way home.

Suddenly she found herself thinking about Taylor again. "You have to stop this," she said to herself, "he's married, and that's that. Forget about him!"

Riley drove home stopping at the mailbox as she pulled into the drive, nothing too thrilling there, same old bills. She went into the house thinking about what she wanted to wear tonight when she visited Tony at work, she had to go, it was the least she could do after disappearing on him the night before. All of a sudden her body began to ache, the tension of the last few days apparently getting to her, she figured a nice warm bath would make her feel better, and definitely keep her going for the next few hours. Riley went into the bathroom, turned on the water and added some bath beads, it would take a few minutes to fill the tub, so she went back to inspect her closet for tonight's outfit.

The bath was wondrous; relaxing and rejuvenating. Riley decided on her black mini-skirt and white blouse, an outfit Tony liked and one that would be perfect for the bar, not overdressed and not too sleazy. It was almost ten o'clock when Riley was ready to leave. Halfway out the door, the phone rang. "Figures," she said as she grabbed the cordless. "Hello?"

"Hey honey, you coming up?"

"Just walking out the door."

"Great! Would you mind picking up a pack of Camels on your way? I'm out and the machine here doesn't stock them."

'That damn cigarette habit,' Riley thought. "Sure," she said. "I'll stop at Mr. Market and grab a pack. I should be at the bar by eleven. See you then."

"Bye." Riley thought more and more about Taylor as she heard Tony's words echoing through her mind. 'Did Taylor smoke?' She wondered. 'If so, what brand?'

It was odd, as she thought more about her relationship with Tony; the more Taylor entered her thoughts.

She had known Tony for over a year and they had been dating for almost as long. It was funny how they met; he bumped into her cart in the local mini-mart. They began to talk and he asked her to join him for dinner the following night, she agreed.

Although she never knew what kept them together, they seemed to be doing all right. No matter what he said or did, they stayed together, Riley managing to keep just enough distance to maintain her independence.

She drove through the Mr. Market parking lot. Finding a spot close to the door; she ran in, bought a pack of Camels and was back in the car just as the raindrops began beating on the windshield.

She drove into the bar parking lot, again looking for a spot close to the door so she would not get soaked by the rain. It seemed futile, so she parked a little further away and waited for the rain to pass. Without thinking, she pulled her cellular phone from its hook and dialed the Squeaky Hinge, asking the bartender what band was playing and until what time. She thanked him for telling her that Taylor and the band would be there until one o'clock. By now the rain had slowed to a drizzle and Riley made a run for the door.

She was greeted by several friends she had met through Tony, as well as a few she knew from living in a small town for many years. They drank and chatted for over an hour. Tony stopped to talk whenever he had a free moment, but since Saturday nights were never slow, they did not do much talking. It was almost midnight when Riley pulled Tony to the side. "I'm tired; I think I'm going to leave."

"Back to our place?"

Riley smiled, this "our place" thing was a new approach he was trying to get her to move in with him.

"Actually, I was going to head back to my place, but I guess I could just pick up some clean clothes and meet you back at your place later." They were talking as they moved towards the front door.

"Deal." He went on to say he should be out of the bar by three; home by 3:15. He leaned over, kissed her lightly on the lips and told her he loved her as he closed the door behind her and went back into the bar.

Love. What a funny word. After all this time, Riley still had a problem uttering those words to Tony. He, however, seemed quite comfortable telling her what he felt. "Just something that takes time" is what Tony said when she told him she was not ready to say "I love you" to him. He said he understood, but sometimes there seemed to be an emptiness after he said something to her and she could not respond in kind.

Riley looked at the clock in her car, the blue numbers read 12:15am. She was tired, and began to debate even going to her house for fresh clothes, she could live in Tony's sweats and T's tomorrow morning while she did a wash. Without thinking about it, she found herself driving north, away from Tony's house.

It was after 12:30 when she pulled into the parking lot at the Squeaky Hinge. 'What am I doing here?' She thought to herself as she pulled into a spot in an unlit area of the lot. For some reason, she felt compelled to drive to the place where, just the night before, she had met a stranger who had since captivated her thoughts.

From where she was parked, Riley could see the back entrance to the bar. It only took a few minutes before the door opened and out came Danny and Taylor along with two other men that Riley recognized as being the drummer and the keyboardist. Within ten minutes, the men had packed up their equipment, said their good-byes and pulled out of the lot. Riley glanced at her clock, the lights, still blue, now said 1:10am. She started the car, pulled out of the lot and began to drive home. Not even a mile down the road, a truck pulled up behind her and began to flash its headlights. Riley, thinking the driver wanted to pass, changed lanes. Surprisingly, so did the truck, still flashing its lights. Riley sped up, hoping to outrun the truck. No such luck, the truck sped up and continued to flash its lights. Without warning, the truck pulled up next to her car. Riley forced herself to keep looking at the road. She did not look at the other driver, who was pacing next to her and now honking the truck's horn.

Finally, she couldn't take it anymore, Riley turned to look at the driver of the truck that had been pacing her for over three miles. It was Taylor! Did he not leave ahead of her? Maybe he came back? But why? Her body was tingling with anticipation as she began to slow down, noting that Taylor did the same. She pulled into a gas station, he followed. Stopping the car, she got out and stood by the door watching him park behind her. He got out and walked towards her.

She felt her stomach flip-flop, what was it about him that was so incredibly appealing? Her eyes were roaming his body as he began to speak.

"Riley Matthews. What brings you out here so late?"

"I was on my way home, thought I'd see if Kim's car was in the parking lot." She was getting too good at lying so easily. "How did you know it was me?"

"Kinda hard to miss your license plate, don't ya think?"

Riley blushed. He was right, that damn plate, Riley 1, was hard to miss, especially with the flashing neon light around it. She made a mental note to take it off tomorrow.

"You mean you don't know anyone else with the same name?"

He smiled. A large grin that showed his beautiful white teeth. "Of course, seeing as Riley is such a common name, and I did see you pull out of the parking lot just a bit ago, what was I thinking, I should have realized it could have been another Riley."

He was sarcastic, but there was something appealing about it. "Ok, I get your point. But why did you stop me?"

Now it was his turn to blush. "You rushed out so quickly last night, I didn't get a chance to say good-bye, and I didn't know if you'd be back again."

Back again? The words echoed in her mind. He wanted to see her again! Married. That was the next word that flashed into her mind. He has a wife and a child. Her little voice was telling her to go home and wait for Tony.

"I hadn't thought about coming back again, I rarely have a free night, and my boyfriend Tony and I usually spend the weekend together."

"Boyfriend? He's a lucky guy." 'Yeah, real lucky,' Riley thought. She was standing in the middle of a parking lot with a married guy she had met only the night before. Tony would not understand. All of a sudden she had a feeling of annoyance. Something told her Taylor was looking for something. Something she was not going to give him, an affair. She missed Tony. Glancing at her watch, Riley realized it was just after 2:30. If she hurried, she could make it home before Tony and he would never have to know.

She turned to Taylor, "Look, I've got to get going. It was nice talking to you, bye."

Taylor watched as she got into the car and closed the door. He leaned over and tapped on the window. Riley took a deep breath and hit the button to make the window go down. As she turned to look at him, he handed her a small piece of paper. "My card. If you ever need to reach me, just call that number."

And with that, he turned, walked back to his truck, got in and disappeared into the night.

Riley put the card into her bag without looking at it. She pushed Taylor to the back of her mind and concentrated on getting home before

Tony. As she drove down the street, she prayed Tony was running late at work.

The clock flashed 3:10 as she turned onto the Oak Ridge Road. Third house on the left, please let there be no car in the driveway. She sighed as she saw the house lights were still as she left them, and Tony's car was not there. Riley rushed into the house, up the stairs, and into the bedroom. She dumped everything on the floor and was climbing into bed as she heard Tony's car pull into the drive. She closed her eyes and said a silent "thank you", as the footsteps came closer to the bedroom.

"Riley? You still awake?" Tony whispered.

"Waiting for you to tuck me in," she teased.

"Tuck you in, huh? I think I'll have to kiss you goodnight first," he said as he climbed into bed and began kissing her.

Riley moaned as she felt his lips slide down her body. She felt herself arch to his touch. It amazed her; he knew exactly what to do and how to do it. Just when it felt like she could not take the arousal any longer, he slid inside of her and they climaxed together.

"I love you, Riley," he whispered in her ear.

The next sound she heard was Tony snoring contentedly. By now he knew better than to wait for Riley to respond in kind. He just rolled over and went to sleep. After all, Riley guessed, why wait for something you don't think is coming? Riley got out of bed and went into the bathroom, closing the door so not to wake Tony with the light.

She splashed cool water on her face. Looking up, she stared at her naked body in the mirror.

"Not too shabby," she said out loud to herself, "guess this is what Tony and Taylor are so interested in."

Riley sat down on top of the plush toilet seat cover and tried to sort through the clutter in her mind. She felt guilty, as if she had cheated on Tony. "But you haven't done anything wrong" was the phrase that kept following her guilty thoughts. Yes, but she had not mentioned anything to Tony about meeting Taylor, or even going to the Squeaky Hinge with Kim the night before.

"Why not," she asked herself. If it was nothing, then why not mention it to Tony? Riley rubbed her temples, the more she tried to rationalize the situation, the more her head pounded. Finally, she gave up, quietly opened the bathroom door, turned out the light and crawled into bed next to Tony.

Chapter 3

Riley awoke to the smell of rain and the sound of thunder. She rubbed her eyes and stretched, reaching over towards Tony. "Morning, sunshine" she heard him say.

"Umm, morning."

"I'm surprised you didn't wake up sooner, the phone has been ringing all morning."

"Oh, anyone interesting?"

"Kevin Greene."

Riley froze. She had not heard that name in several months and could have gone the rest of her lifetime without ever hearing it again.

Blinking back tears, Riley looked at Tony, "did you talk to him?"

Tony reached over and took her hand. "No, I told him to leave the number and if you were interested in speaking with him, you would call him. I told him if he did not hear from you, he was not to call again. Number's by the phone."

"Thanks," was about all she could say. "I'm gonna jump into the shower." "You okay?"

"I'll be fine. Just need some time to think." Riley climbed out of bed, grabbed a fresh towel from the closet and went into the bathroom. It had been almost two years ago and although Tony knew about her parents' death, she had never talked about her parents with him. He never asked. She knew he realized that when she was ready, she would talk, until then, he let her mourn in her own way and she was grateful for that.

As the hot water hit her skin, tears began to run down her cheeks. Within moments, Riley was overcome with memories of the past. The memory was still so clear in her mind. It was late summer and her parents were returning from the house on the Cape where they had spent every summer since Riley was born. Riley had spent the summer as an intern and could not take the trip to the Cape, so her parents went alone which left Riley at their Manalapan Estate with the help.

At three a.m. the phone rang, Riley vaguely remembered hearing it ring, but the sound of Maria's screams would echo through her mind forever. Riley ran to Maria, grabbed the phone out of her hands and asked the person on the other end to repeat what they had said.

The voice began to speak and the words became a blur, ".... Matthews' plane.....crashed......no survivors...very sorry for your loss."

To this day, Riley could not remember who was on the other end of that phone, saying her parent's plane had crashed and no one had survived. She remembers the phone being taken from her hand, someone hugging her and then a room full of her parent's friends and associates rushing about in a crowded home that had always seemed so large for the three of them and their small staff while Riley was growing up. Maria stayed on for a while after the crash, but within a few months, the absence of Mr. and Mrs. Matthews got to her and she went back to Venezuela to be with her family. Riley was left alone with only Sam, the caretaker, and his wife still living on the property. Then came the fateful day when Kevin Greene walked into her life. He was a lawyer, representing others on the Matthews' chartered plane. His goal was to prove that the plane had not been inspected as it should have been by the maintenance company and the forty people who died that day might be alive today if the plane was taken care of properly. He wanted to sue the company for wrongful death and negligence, on behalf of the survivors.

When he first contacted her, Riley was polite and agreed to meet with him to hear what he had to say. After the first meeting though, Riley had the distinct impression that this man did not care about the surviving family members of those on flight 675 from Massachusetts to Palm Beach, he was only interested in receiving his cut of the settlement, hoping to make himself enough to retire on. Riley told him she appreciated his inquiry, but was not going to commit herself to a lawsuit, she had her parents' lawyers to handle her affairs, and felt it was in her best interest to leave things the way they were. Basically, "thanks, but no thanks."

She had heard from Kevin a couple of times over the past two years, checking to see if she had changed her mind and wanted to be part of the suit, but he had not called in the past six months and she had hoped it was over.

Her parents' estate had long been settled. Since she was the only living heir there was no one to contest the will and everything was changed into Riley's name and she went on with her life. It was lonely for a while, and she still found herself talking to her parents when things got tough, but all in all, with Tony's support over the past year, things had gotten better. Now this. What did Kevin want after all this time?

Riley took a deep breath, stood under the shower, allowing the water to splash over her face. "Time to get a grip on things," she said to herself. She felt her body relax, tension floating away. She rinsed off and climbed out; grabbing the towel she had left on the counter. As she dried off, her thoughts were becoming clearer. Her mind was focusing on the future for the first time since her parents' death. She looked in the mirror at her tear-stained face and smiled, realizing there was something she needed to do.

The cool air hit her as she opened the bathroom door. Tony was lying on the bed, channel surfing with the remote. He looked up at her and smiled, "you okay?"

Riley did not say a word as she walked towards him, taking the remote from his hands and clicking the set off. She could feel his eyes watching her as she dropped her towel to the floor. He smiled, and she could sense his excitement, he started to say something, she placed her finger over his lips, her eyes meeting his. She straddled his waist, gently kissing his lips.

He put his hands on her back, and then slid them down to her hips, grabbing her firmly and positioning her so he could slide inside her at any given moment. Riley was not giving up control that easily. She reached behind her and took his hands in hers. She kissed him harder, took hold of his wrists and pinned them down to the bed over his head. Tony looked surprised, but as Riley felt his hardness grow, she knew he was enjoying everything she was doing. At that moment, she slid him inside of her and rode him with an intensity they had never shared before. Tony screamed out loud as he climaxed with her. Their chests pounding and bodies sweating, they held each other tightly as their climax ended. Tony stroked her hair, chuckled and said, "guess your shower was a waste." Riley picked her head up from his chest and looked him in the eyes smiling, "not true, it helped me to realize something."

"Oh, and what might that have been?" He asked sarcastically.

"I love you."

Tony smiled. She had never seen him smile like that before. His eyes lit up as he said, "I'm glad you can finally say that. I love you too." He reached over and took her in his arms and held her tightly.

Riley never called Kevin Greene back; instead she had her father's attorney serve Kevin with papers ordering him to stay away from her permanently. Riley had finally put the past behind her, and was moving forward, full speed ahead.

The following weekend, she and Tony packed up her apartment and moved everything into his house. At first, her landlord was hesitant to let her break the lease, but a few dollars and a choice bottle of scotch changed his mind quickly enough.

By the time Saturday evening rolled around, they were sitting in front of the TV watching HBO and eating pizza in their new home. Every now and then Riley felt Tony watching her; she turned to find him staring at her, his happiness apparent through his sparkling eyes.

"I'm glad you're here," he said.

"Me too. I think it's time we get on with our lives. I don't know if I've ever thanked you for everything you have seen me through, I really appreciate it."

He moved closer to her, putting his arm around her, "Riley, I love you and I have since the day we bumped carts in the grocery store. I knew right off that something was going on in your life, something you needed to settle before we could move on. I was always willing to wait for you, I want to spend the rest of my life with you, and nothing could ever change that feeling."

Riley felt the tears come to her eyes as she leaned over and kissed him gently on the cheek, "I want us to grow old together. Thank you for having the patience to wait for me." He kissed her softly on her forehead as she rested her head on his shoulder. Within moments, she was sleeping soundly.

The next few weeks passed by without incident. Living with Tony was peaceful for Riley, she enjoyed waking up with him and from what he said, he enjoyed seeing her next to him when he went to sleep and when he awoke. All in all, things were going well.

As things began to settle, Riley decided to redecorate. Tony had given her his blessing and decided to stay out of it. "Do whatever you'd like; I trust your judgment and taste."

At first, Riley thought she would do the whole house in one swift movement, but as she became more involved with redecorating, she found working on one room at a time to be the best approach. With the living room and kitchen plans done, she decided her next step would be the deck. Over the years, it had gone from clean and beautiful with wood trim to blotchy and tattered from the rain and sun. Although he had turned the redecorating over to her she was not sure how Tony would react to her idea of taking everything out of the area and putting in a concrete garden area, but she figured dinner and some wine might put him in an agreeable mood.

Dinner was planned perfectly; a couple of filets, fresh cooked vegetables and baked potatoes, along with a bottle of wine, Tony might actually give in to the garden idea.

"Hey, Riley, I'm home," he shouted as the front door closed, "you here?"

"In here, honey."

"Ummm, something smells good, what's for dinner?"

"I made your favorite, hopefully you're hungry?"

"I could eat the side of a house, I'm so hungry. Never got to take a break for lunch. Last thing my stomach saw was a pop-tart or two around 9am this morning."

"Good, then let's eat."

Tony grabbed some dishes from the cabinet. Riley grabbed the wine and a couple of glasses, and they sat down.

They ate and drank, Riley waiting for the perfect moment to ask him about redoing the deck area. Finally, she thought she had the moment, but instead Tony put down his fork and turned to her with a big grin on his face.

"What are you smiling about?'

"I was just thinking about how much I enjoy being with you."

"I know that, I enjoy being with you too. Actually, I have something I want to ask you about."

"Riley, can it wait? I have something I need to ask you first."

Riley was a little uneasy with his comment, but figured she would roll with the punches. "Sure, hon, what is it?"

Tony stood up, walked over and knelt down next to her chair, turning her towards him. Riley, surprised by his actions, stared at him without saying a word.

He took her hand in his, looked up at her and said, "Riley, I love you, will you do me the honor of being my wife?" He opened the black jewelry box he was holding, inside was a beautiful diamond ring, he took out the ring, placed the box on the table and took her hand in his, "will you marry me?"

Riley looked at Tony, his deep green eyes, dark wavy hair and a lean muscular body on top of that wonderful personality, she could not be more flattered that he was asking her to be his wife. Her smile lit up her tear-stained face as she answered him, "yes, I will marry you Tony."

He slipped the ring onto her finger, kissed her hand gently, stood up and took her in his arms. For the first time since her parents' death, Riley felt complete again, her feet were on solid ground, and she was looking forward to her life with Tony.

Riley still wanted to redo the outside patio and found her opportunity to approach Tony with the idea a few days later at breakfast. "Honey, what do you think about redoing the patio area?"

Tony looked puzzled. "Define redoing."

"You know, taking up the rocks and stones and putting down concrete, covered with tiles. Then we could put a table and some chairs out there, maybe get some big plants for the corners. Make the area more usable. It wouldn't cost that much, and we could probably hire someone to do the job within a few days' time."

"Riley, you amaze me. We have an entire wedding to plan, including picking a date, and you want to first start on the patio?"

"Tony, the wedding is not that big a deal to plan. If there was one thing my mother taught me, it was never plan a big party on your own, always hire someone who knows what they are doing to plan it for you. It may cost a little more, but in the end it will be well worth it. Those are her words exactly."

Tony looked at her. "I think this might be a good time to bring up something I think we should discuss."

"Sure, what's up?"

"Well, I was raised to believe that the man should be the main breadwinner in the family, I know your parents' death left you provided for. I just think that since we're going to be spending our lives together; maybe we should sit down and discuss our financial plans."

Riley was not surprised. In fact, she had expected this for quite some time, if anything she was rather surprised that it had taken so long to be brought up.

"Tony, I was raised in a home where, even though my dad was the main breadwinner, my mom had her own things to occupy her time. She was successful in her own way, and even though she didn't work for financial gain, she worked hard to achieve her goals. I was taught to work hard for everything I wanted and if there came a time that I was financially secure, to enjoy what I had, and share it with those I love. The sad truth is that my parents' death left me more financially secure than I could have ever imagined. However, I had thought about working part-time, or volunteering to keep myself involved and when we start our family, that's when I would focus on the family stuff.

Quite frankly, neither one of us will ever want for anything in a monetary sense again, but that doesn't mean we can't set goals to achieve. What do you think?"

"I agree. I just wanted to make sure you understood, that I am not interested in you for your money, I love you for the person that you are. "

"Tony, I know that."

"Good."

"Now that we have that settled, what do you think of my idea?"

"Which one? The wedding planner or the patio?"

"Both."

"Well, the wedding planner is fine, but I just want to make sure that this isn't someone who plans things without our ok. She just gives us ideas and we have the final say, right?"

"Of course."

"Then okay to the planner idea. As for the patio, let me think on it for a while. I want to redo it, but I'd feel better about it if I handled it. That okay with you?"

"Sure, knock yourself out. I'll set my sights on planning the wedding. Any input on the date, Mr. groom-to-be?"

"No, just don't make it on a holiday like Super-bowl Sunday or something. That would not be a good thing."

Riley laughed. "Since when has Super-bowl Sunday become a holiday?"

"Well, it may not be a national holiday, but let me give you forewarning hon, I'll be watching the Superbowl, so if you plan our wedding on that day, let's just say you'll be short one groom."

Tony apparently didn't see the chair cushion come flying at him as he left the dining room, but Riley heard him grunt as he felt it hit his head. "That's what you get for being a pain in my butt!" she shouted after him.

"I love you too!"

She heard him close the garage door.

Riley spent the next few weeks dragging Kim from store to store trying on wedding gowns and veils. At just the right moment, Riley asked Kim to stand up for her as her maid of honor.

"Riley, I would be so proud, I..." her words trailed off as the tears ran down Kim's face. Riley had not realized how much her marrying Tony would affect her best friend. They continued to walk along the avenue, looking in store windows, as Kim composed herself.

Riley began to reflect on her past and for the first time thought about how her parents would have reacted to her wedding.

"My little girl is getting married," Riley could almost hear her mother's voice uttering those words and could also picture her father standing next to the mantle, pipe in hand, saying, "Riley, Riley, Riley, it's time for you to go off and start your own family now..."

Her parents would be so proud of her. Although Tony would not necessarily be the man of their dreams, they would accept him because she loved him, but did she?

Suddenly she caught herself. 'What are you thinking Riley, of course you love Tony, why else would you have agreed to marry him?' Riley's mind began to race, more cluttered than ever before and just when she could take the pressure no more, she grabbed her head and cried out, "stop it, stop it, stop it!!!"

"Stop what?" asked Kim.

Riley opened her eyes and realized she was still with Kim walking along the avenue.

"Riley, stop what?" Kim asked again, this time clearly agitated.

"Oh, nothing, I just couldn't figure out what type of cake we should have and you know how I am, my mind started racing and, well I just got a little carried away. I'm fine, let's head home though; I'm not really in the mood to look at dresses anymore today."

"You know what we need, Riley?"

"What?"

"We need a girl's night out, party hardy, like we used to. In fact, let's go to the Squeaky Hinge! What do you think? We'll go out tonight!"

Riley thought for a minute, maybe she did need to get out and have some fun for a change. Things had slowed down on the party circuit since she and Tony had moved in together. Her late night trips to visit him at the bar were no longer necessary, and she really had not made much of an effort to meet him after work lately, since he usually just came home. Maybe a night out would do her some good.

"Okay, the Squeaky Hinge it is," she said.

It was after nine when Riley pulled into the parking lot of the Squeaky Hinge Bar. She looked for Kim's car as she walked towards to door of the restaurant. Kim was waiting inside in by the hostess stand; she smiled as Riley came in. "You won't believe this, guess who's playing here tonight?"

Kim did not even wait for Riley to take a guess, "Danny's band!" she blurted out as she thrust a brightly colored flyer into Riley's hand. Riley turned the paper over and glanced briefly at the photo of Taylor and his band leaning against their instruments.

Kim was obviously very excited at seeing Danny again, although Riley could not imagine why. She decided against saying anything more than, "oh, what a coincidence" as she shoved the flyer into her bag.

The band was playing when they sat down. They sat close to the stage, just out of direct range of the speakers, since neither Kim nor Riley had the desire to be deaf by the end of the night.

It only took a few songs before his voice came over the sound system. "This next song is for a very special brown-eyed girl." That was all Riley had to hear, it was enough to make her turn around and look directly at the stage, where she saw Taylor smiling at her as the song began.

Before the song ended Kim headed towards the ladies room which left Riley alone to hear the announcement of the band taking a break. Next thing she knew, Taylor was sitting down across from her in Kim's empty chair.

"Riley Matthews, my brown-eyed girl. What brings you out tonight? And without the boyfriend no less..." Riley stared at Taylor as he spoke. His voice was smooth and clear, his eyes twinkled and his smile melted her heart.

What was she thinking, she was engaged to be married soon, and Taylor was married already. With that thought, she glanced at his hand only to notice his ring was gone! Where was it? She wanted to ask, but what, how?

"Riley? You okay?" He asked.

It took a moment, but Riley snapped out of her daze and realized that Taylor was talking to her. "You okay?" He asked again.

"Yeah, fine, guess my mind was wondering. Sorry."

"Not a problem. I was going to step outside for some fresh air, care to join me?"

"I'd love to," Riley heard herself say as she stood up to walk outside.

Riley followed him out the back door and into the cool night air. At first she thought they were going to sit outside the door. When Taylor did not stop, she asked, "where are we going?"

"Oh, I thought we would walk around to the back where we could have some privacy. I didn't mean to make you uncomfortable."

"Not at all, just curious as to where we were heading."

Taylor stopped alongside a bench leaning against the backside of the building. There was not another soul in sight, although the stereo from inside the bar could be heard.

"Have a seat, my beautiful brown-eyed girl," he said and extended his arm, palm open and face up pointing towards the bench.

Riley hesitated a moment before sitting down on the beach. She cocked her head slightly before relaxing into a smile and patting the seat next to her with her hand, "won't you join me?" she asked.

"With pleasure." He took a seat next to her.

They talked for a few moments. Taylor leaned over and placed his hand on Riley's cheek, gently stroking her face, then he leaned over and kissed her. At first Riley was surprised, he was so gentle she was unsure of how to respond, but then she found herself kissing him back, very passionately.

Suddenly, she pulled away from him, "Taylor, I can't do this, you're married!"

For what seemed to be an eternity, Taylor stared at her. Then softly, he spoke. "Riley, my wife and I have split up. She's back in Detroit with her family. It became obvious that we want different things out of life and unfortunately, there is no way to resolve our differences."

Now it was Riley's turn to stare at him. "Are you serious?"

"Very much so. And maybe I'm wrong, but I felt something very powerful when we first met, so when you showed up tonight I couldn't help but act on my instincts. I'm very sorry if I've offended you in any way…that was not my intention."

This time Riley leaned over and kissed him, her passion obvious. Taylor responded in kind, for at that moment, their passion and desire for each other was all that mattered.

Break time passed very quickly, and Taylor had one more set to play. "Will you wait for me, I'd like to talk some more, if that's okay with you?"

Chapter 4

Riley smiled, "sure, I'll wait."

With that she headed back toward the table where Kim was in the midst of men fawning over her southern drawl and California girl looks. As Riley approached the table the pack seemed to magically disburse. Kim looked up inquisitively.

"Where have you been and what is that silly grin on your face?" Kim asked.

"I went outside for some air and I guess it did me more good than I thought," she lied, but right now, Riley had no desire to share her experience with Kim. She needed time to figure out what to do, not to mention thinking of a way to get Kim to leave before her, so she could wait and talk with Taylor.

"Hey, Kim, I think it's getting late, why don't we head out?" Riley hoped Kim would not mind leaving before the band stopped playing.

"Are you sure you don't want to stay a little longer? It'll be a long time before you get another girls' night out, soon you'll be an old married woman..."

Kim could not have known how much her words stung. Riley tried her best to laugh as she said, "oh, not to worry, I'll be the first old married party girl. I promise we'll get out as much as we always did."

"In that case, let's head out." Kim flagged the waitress for the check. Pushing Riley's money back at her as she tried to pay her share, "this was my idea, my treat, no arguing."

Riley was too excited to argue. The band was almost at the end of their set and she had to get Kim out the door and herself back to the bar quickly.

"Let's go, Kim!" She headed out the door.

Kim chased behind. "Wait up, Riley, what's your hurry?"

"No hurry, just want to beat the traffic."

"Whatever." Kim was clearly annoyed, but as far as Riley was concerned, she had more important things to concern herself with.

Riley breathed a sigh of relief when Kim pulled out of the parking lot and onto the main road. Confident Kim would not look back, Riley turned off her headlights and cut the engine. Glancing at her watch, she realized Taylor would be coming outside very soon.

Bright flashing lights brought Riley out of her daze and back to the parking lot. Squinting, she made out the figure of Taylor sitting behind the wheel of his truck parked in front of her. She stepped out of her car as he rolled down his window.

"Let's go for a ride" he said.

She smiled as she hopped into the passenger seat of the truck, not once thinking about her parents' warning her as a child never to get in a car with a stranger; for some reason, he seemed so familiar, almost as if she had known him all of her life.

"Where are we headed?"

"I thought we'd drive up the coast a bit, I know this little area where all the fisherman hang out."

"Taylor, it's after one in the morning, somehow I doubt there will be people fishing."

He laughed a warm, caring laugh. Riley watched his blue eyes sparkle as he smiled. It was hard to understand why he and his wife would split up; he was such a warm and loving man. 'She must be foolish,' was the thought that ran through Riley's mind as they drove off into the night.

As they pulled into the inlet, Taylor rolled down the windows and the smell of sea air filled the truck. He was right about the fishermen, the pier was full. The surprising thing was that there were not only men, but families; mothers, fathers and children of all ages sharing in the fishing experience. Riley was mesmerized, her mind wondering back to when she and her parents would take their boat out and fish in the middle of the ocean. It had been a long time since she had smelled fresh sea air, the aroma of fish, and the sound of rods being cast. Taylor came around to the passenger side of the truck, taking her hand as she climbed out. She looked at him and smiled as they began to walk hand in hand onto the pier.

The night air was brisk, the sky a dark black sheet of stars. They walked along the pier until they found an open bench to sit. Without a word, Taylor sat and put his arm around her, Riley found herself relaxing, her eyes closed, she leaned back breathing in the night air. Taylor stroked her hair and gently kissed her head.

Her mind began to wander. She had so many questions she wanted to ask, but where, how to begin?

Almost as if he had read her mind, Taylor whispered softly to her, "I feel as if I've known you all of my life, yet I know nothing about you..."

She smiled, "I was just thinking that very thought. Tell me about yourself, I want to know all about you. I don't even know how old you are..."

"Thirty-one. Is that too old for you, my lovely lady?"

"Well, my cut-off is usually thirty, but for you I'll make an exception," she said laughing.

"Thank you. I'm not sure what I would have done if you chose not to hang out with an old guy like me."

"You are far from old. Now, if you don't mind, I'd like to hear the Taylor story."

"Very well, my sweet, where shall I begin?" He stroked his chin as if deep in thought.

"Taylor, come on!" Riley jokingly smacked him on his stomach.

"Okay, okay, here goes. I was born and raised in Alabama, the youngest of three children. I moved to Detroit to go to college, originally I studied psychology..."

"You were a psych major?" Riley sat up and laughed, Taylor certainly did not strike her as the Freudian type.

"Do you want to hear my story or not?"

"Yes, I'm sorry, go on." She leaned her head back and cuddled up against his chest.

"Now, as I was saying, I was a psych major, but then the local high school had an internship open for a broadcast instructor; somehow I was talked into taking it. Next thing I knew, I was in love with broadcasting and switched majors. Anyway, I did a bunch of odd jobs over the next few years, and finally graduated.

"How did you end up in Florida?"

"Relax, I'm getting there. While I was in Detroit I answered an ad about a local band. Anyway, I played with them for a while, but there were some problems when the lead singer's wife began flirting with me."

For a moment there was silence, Riley opened her eyes and looked up at him. "Why did you stop?"

"Just lost my train of thought for a moment, sorry. So, like I was saying, this woman was making passes at me, and it was getting out of hand. I finally decided to leave the band and head south for a change of pace. I was here about two months when she showed up on my front step."

"The woman from Detroit?"

"Yep."

"You've got to be kidding me, what did she want?"

"Me."

Riley was now sitting straight up and staring at him in disbelief. "She came all the way from Detroit to see you?"

"Well, she had more serious things in mind."

Amazing, she never thought Taylor would be so interesting, she figured him for the typical "met my college sweetheart, got married, got bored type" apparently she was wrong.

"Then what happened?" He had her attention now.

"Well, she told me that she was lost without me and had to be with me. Actually, she scared me at first, but then I realized she was just lost, lonely and sad, but not harmful. Since it was late and there was nowhere else for her to go, I let her stay on my couch for the weekend. By the end of the weekend the rest of the story came out. Apparently, she had left her husband and kids and had no intention of going back. She begged me to let her stay with me until she got situated, and I agreed."

"Wow that was not what I expected to hear."

"Oh, it gets better. When she arrived, I had a bit of a problem with..." his voice trailed off.

"Problem with what?" She asked.

"Let's just say that I was not exactly sober most of the time. I spent a lot of time either drunk or high. And she took advantage of it. Not to say I was not a willing partner, just that the precautions I would have taken normally, I didn't take. So the outcome was she got pregnant."

It hit her like a load of bricks, "are you telling me Jeni was that woman? And you married her because she was pregnant with your daughter?"

His eyes had lost their shine, "that's exactly what I'm saying. Once she was pregnant I knew I had an obligation to do the right thing. So we were married a few months later, as soon as her divorce was finalized. I stopped using drugs and cleaned up my act; got a full-time job and nine months later Kelsey was born."

Amazed was not even strong enough to describe what she was feeling. "Wow!" was all she could say. "I don't know what to say."

"I guess that was not the Taylor story you were expecting?"

"Far from it, kinda figured you for the "married-my-high- school-sweetheart-type" never thought of a "obsessive-girlfriend-gets-pregnant-trapped-into-marriage" story. You're definitely full of surprises, that's for sure."

He held her tightly, "Riley, I hope now that you know more about me, you'll still give me a chance. Jeni and I are going through a tough time, but once the paperwork is final, the marriage will be over and I can move on. I'd really like to get to know you better, but I'll understand if you think this is all too much to handle, it is quite a mess."

She moved closer into his arms, "Taylor, I don't scare that easily. I'll stick around for a bit and we can go from there. But for now, I've got to get home, it's really late." Riley had been so intent on listening to his story she had totally lost track of time. Panic struck her and she jumped up, "let's get going."

Suddenly her life came flooding back to her, she had a wonderful fiancée' waiting at home for her, and if he hadn't started to worry by now, he would soon.

Taylor took her hand and they began to walk back to his truck. He opened the door for her and she climbed in. Before closing it, he leaned over and gently kissed her on the mouth, "I don't know what I did to deserve meeting you, but I feel very lucky." And with that he closed the door.

Riley glanced at the clock on the dash, it was after three in the morning, Tony was going to be upset, and going home was not something she was looking forward to. Taylor climbed into the truck and they drove back down the coast to the Squeaky Hinge. As they pulled into the parking lot, Riley felt her stomach turn, she did not want to leave him, yet she knew she had to.

He parked next to her car, got out and walked over to the passenger side to let her out. As he took her hand to help her step out from the cab he said, "Riley, I would like to see you again. Is it okay for me to call you?"

She thought for a moment, then reached into her purse, took out a piece of paper and scribbled her cell phone number on it.

"You can reach me at this number" she said as she handed him the paper. "I've got to go now." She kissed him gently, walked to her car, climbed in and drove off into the night without looking back.

Taylor stood in the parking lot for a moment, staring at her car as she drove away, "what in the world are you doing?" he asked himself out loud. He had no idea that the person sitting in the truck watching him from across the parking lot was asking the very same question.

Chapter 5

Riley had never driven so fast in all of her life. She made it back to town in record time, and without even thinking headed down Main Street past all of the late night bars. As she came to the light, she glanced to the parking lot on her left and then took a double take as she realized that Tony's car was parked in front of Smiley's Pub. A sigh of relief escaped her, he hadn't been home yet! Tony must have gone out after work. She was safe, he didn't know she wasn't home.

'Oh thank God!' was the only thought that crossed Riley's mind. It was safe for her to head home. The light changed and Riley made her turn, never looking back to see the dark colored sport utility truck make the same turn behind her.

The porch light was still on when she pulled into the driveway, what a relief. Her head was no longer pounding with a stress headache, although every bone and muscle in her body was sore. The tension was too much, she had not thought about the consequences that would await her when she came home from meeting with Taylor. Now that she did not have to face them, a whole new set of problems arose. She parked the car and headed into the house. As she walked through the front door, she was struck by the stillness of the house. Nothing seemed familiar to her, almost as though she was entering a stranger's home. "This is silly," her own voice startled her as she spoke out loud. She reached over and flipped on the lights for the stairs, "that's better."

Just as she was about to head upstairs, Riley noticed the red light on the answering machine flashing at her. "Play-me, Play-me," it seemed to say in time with the flashing light. Riley pushed the play button. As the machine rewound itself she sat down on the chair and kicked off her shoes.

Message one was from Kim, did she get home okay? Oh well, too late to call her back on that one. The next few messages were from an assortment of Tony's buddies, all wanting to know if he was heading out after his shift. The next message was from Tony, letting her know that he would be meeting friends at Smiley's pub, not too worry and of course, she was more than welcome to join them. How lucky am I? That was the first thought to cross her mind, this kind man calls me to let me know where he is so I won't worry and what do I do? I go out and spend the evening with some guy on the fishing pier! "Never again!" Riley said out loud to herself, he's too good a guy to deserve this.

Riley was almost totally lost in her own promises that she almost missed the last message. In fact she replayed it three times just to be able to hear it clearly. "I know where you've been, leave him alone" was all the woman's voice said. Riley froze. Who could that be? More importantly, what did it mean? She reached over and scrolled through the callers on the ID box. That's odd, the call that matched the message on the machine came from a payphone. Who would call her from a payphone just to leave a crank message?

Riley erased the messages, and the numbers on the ID box, but not before jotting down the payphone number. She made a mental note to herself to call the phone company in the morning to find out where the payphone was located.

Right now it's time to get some sleep, she thought, especially since Tony wasn't home yet. She could at least have the bed to herself for a while. She turned out the lights and climbed the stairs, with each step her body seemed to be slowing down, her desire to climb into a soft bed was growing stronger by the step. She headed into the bedroom, flipped the switch on the wall and illuminated the room with light. What a mess, clothes everywhere, on the floor, on the chair and most of all, on the stair stepper. Need to use that thing more often, she said as she pulled off her clothes and tossed them into a pile on the floor in front of the machine.

Staring at her body in the mirror, Riley noticed she was not as well defined as she had been. "Time to get back into the gym," she said out loud. Maybe that will help clear my mind, maybe if I spend more time working out and getting my body stronger, my mind will follow. Who knows, maybe my chaotic life will actually begin to make sense. As her mind began to race with jumbled thoughts Riley fell onto the bed and closed her eyes, hoping to stop herself from thinking, she needed to relax. Her yoga and meditation classes came back to her mind and without even thinking about it; she began breathing from her diaphragm, belly breathing, that's what her instructor called it; deep and cleansing breaths, relaxing the mind as well as the body. Riley was so involved in her breathing exercise she did not hear Tony pull into the driveway or come into the house. It was not until he was in the bedroom that she realized he was there.

"Tony?"

"Hey, didn't mean to wake you."

"That's okay, how was Smiley's?"

"Would have been better if you were there."

"Sorry, I was just too tired when I got back, I needed to get some sleep," she lied. This was not a good thing; she seemed to be getting too good at creating stories at the drop of a hat. 'What is with you Riley Matthews,' she asked herself. Lying was not her style, yet lately she had become not only good at it, but she found herself doing it more and more.

"Everyone asked about you, I told them you were probably at home, just not in the mood to go out." It was almost as if he knew she hadn't been home, but was not going to come right out and ask her.

She felt the need to change the subject before things became more complicated. "Yeah, that's about it. You coming to bed honey?"

She propped herself up on her elbows, watching him get undressed. He seemed to be focused on something else. She asked him if he was okay.

"Yeah, fine," was the response she received.

Couldn't figure him out sometimes, something must have put him in a mood, she guessed. She knew his mind was on something else, she wondered what it could be, yet her mind never thought that very moment he was trying to understand how she could have been home for hours and yet the hood of her car was still hot to the touch. Figuring it was best to leave it alone for now, he finished undressing and climbed into bed next to her, hoping a good night's sleep would calm his restless mood. As soon as he lay down he realized sleep was not going to happen right away, Riley had something else in mind, but as she began to touch him, he couldn't help but think that she had someone else on her mind as well.

Tony had a very sexy body, but then again, so did Taylor. She wondered what Taylor was like in bed, aggressive or maybe passive? She was still in the midst of her fantasy when Tony climbed into bed next to her. Even though she knew it was wrong, she began making love to Tony, fantasizing about Taylor as she stroked him. She kissed him. His response was almost mechanical, but Riley never noticed. In her mind she was kissing Taylor, running her hands down his back, her arms wrapped tightly around him as he entered her.

Their lovemaking was short but satisfying. Tony was asleep in moments, his snoring echoing through the room.

Riley lay in bed, her eyes fixated on the ceiling fan as it circled. She could not get past her desire to be with Taylor. What is so appealing about him? Asking herself this over and over again, she still had not answered herself as she drifted off to sleep.

When she awoke the next morning, Tony was gone. She glanced at the clock; it was only ten thirty, where could he be? She grabbed a T-shirt and headed downstairs.

"Tony," she called, but there was no response. She walked through the house, ending up in the kitchen where she found a note taped to the refrigerator, "gone out, back later" was all it said. Short and to the point. She crumbled it up and tossed it into the wastebasket, wondering what that was all about. Tony was not one for such curt notes, and even if he's in a hurry he always signs them "love me."

She couldn't help but think back to last night, he seemed out of sorts, his mind was somewhere else, but what or who was he thinking about? Oh well, nothing she could do about it until he came home. She thought about things for a moment, then realized she and Tony hadn't spent much quality time together lately. Maybe that's what they needed. More specifically, maybe it would help her to clarify her thoughts and straighten things out.

She surveyed the fridge, not much in the way of dinner in there. "Guess you're heading to the market," she said out loud. Grabbing a soda from the door, she turned and headed upstairs to get dressed.

Forty minutes later Riley was driving down State Road 56, heading towards the mini-mart. The lot was almost empty, so she parked closed to the exit door, threw her purse over her shoulder and headed inside. She roamed the isles in search of something special, something different, after all she did want this to be a nice evening and bad food can spoil any evening. She decided on swordfish, fresh vegetables and baked potatoes for the main course, reminding herself to stop at the bakery next door on the way out for dessert. As she made her way to the checkout stand, she added two scented candles and a bottle of wine to her cart. The thing she liked best about the mini-mart is that she could be in and out of there very quickly.

She stopped at the bakery and after ten minutes of debating between a double chocolate mousse with strawberries and a marble cheesecake with raspberries, she paid the salesgirl for both of them, took her change and left the store.

She put the packages into the trunk, climbed into the car, turned up the radio, pulled out of the parking lot and onto State Road 56. As she pulled into the driveway her cell phone began to ring. She was about to let the call go to voicemail when she remembered she had given the number to Taylor. She reached over and pulled the phone from her purse, she took a deep breathe and pushed the talk button.

"Hello?"

"Riley? I was trying to reach Tony." It was Shawn, Tony's boss.

"Shawn? You must have dialed me by...." Riley's stomach turned as the words came out of her mouth. "What number did you dial?"

He answered as if she was asking him a stupid question, "I dialed Tony's cell number, 525-0545, is he there?"

"Sorry Shawn, I must have picked up Tony's phone by mistake," she tried to stay calm as she realized that if she had his phone, he had hers and Taylor had the number.

"Not a big deal, just tell him he's off tonight and on Friday."

"Sure, I'll tell him."

"Thanks, bye."

"Bye," she said as she pushed the red button on the phone. Riley stared at the phone for a moment, then dialed her cell phone number and pushed the send button. All she heard was silence at first, then the ringing began.

"Hello?" It was a Tony.

"Hey you, where'd you head off to so early," she tried to keep her voice light; she did not want him to think something was up.

"Had a few errands to run before work tonight, wanted to get an early start."

"Where are you?" Please be close by she prayed.

"Actually, I'm about two miles from the house, I should be there soon. Where are you?"

She breathed a sigh of relief. "I'm home, and I have a surprise, I'll see you in a few minutes."

"Okay, bye." He hung up before she could respond in kind. She dropped the phone back into her purse and opened the door. The Florida humidity hit her quickly, nothing like a Florida summer. By noon the air was so thick people could hardly breathe. Pushing her bangs off her face, she grabbed the packages and headed for the front door.

The cool air hit her as she walked through the door. Dropping the packages on the counter, Riley glanced at the answering machine. The red light was flashing, one message, she looked at the ID box before hitting the play button. The message was from Kim wondering why she had not called her back last night. Riley scolded herself for forgetting to return the call, usually she was not so forgetful, but lately her mind had been so cluttered half the time she couldn't remember which end was up. She dialed Kim's number as she unpacked and put away the groceries.

Kim answered almost immediately. "Hello?"

"Kim? Hey, it's me."

"Riley, what's up? Why didn't you call me last night?"

"Sorry, I got in and went straight to bed, never heard the phone." There she went again, now she was not only lying to Tony, but to her best friend as well.

"Oh, no big deal." Kim brushed it off like it was nothing. Riley was grateful that Kim was not one to hold a grudge or to ask too many questions, right now Riley couldn't understand what she was going through let alone try to explain it to someone else.

"Listen, Tony just pulled in and I have a surprise for him, so I really have to go. I'll call you later, okay?"

"Sure, later." They said their good-byes and Riley hung up the phone as Tony came through the front door.

"Riley, you forgot to close the trunk" he called out.

"Oops. Sorry, will you close it for me please?" She laughed as she reminded herself to remember not to be so forgetful.

"Did already," was the next thing she heard him say as he came into the kitchen. "What's this?" He asked pointing to the empty bakery boxes on the counter.

"Your surprise. I'm making us dinner tonight, something romantic and quiet since we really haven't had much time together."

"Riley, I have to work tonight and don't you have a..." he stopped in mid sentence as if rethinking his next comment.

"Actually, you don't have to work tonight. Shawn called and said you're off tonight and working tomorrow. So that's taken care of, and I don't know what you thought I was doing tonight, but I haven't made any plans." She paused a moment as they stared at each other. Something was up. He was looking at her with a sarcastic look on his face, almost daring her to keep talking. "Tony, what's up? Finish your sentence, what is it you thought I was doing tonight?"

"Quite frankly, I thought you had a date."

"A date? What on earth are you talking about?" She tried to read him, but the look on his face was a mixture of anger and hurt. Most importantly, she had no idea what he was referring to.

"Well, first you disappeared last night and lied to me about it and then today I have gotten a few hang up calls on the cell phone. At first I thought nothing of it, but then again I didn't realize I had your phone. So now I'm thinking that you were out with someone you don't want me to know about and therefore I'm not exactly in the best of moods. Okay? Does that satisfy your curiosity?"

She had never heard him so upset; she was not sure how to respond. "What do you mean about last night? I was here."

"You told me you came home and went to sleep, but your car was still hot when I got in, so you obviously did not come straight home."

"You're right, after Kim and I went out we came back here and talked for a while, we started watching a movie and I drove her home when it ended. So, yes, the car was probably still hot because I had dropped Kim off not too long before you got home. As for the hang-up phone calls, I have no idea who that could be. Tony, I love you and I would never jeopardize our relationship for anyone or anything." Her words sounded sincere even to her, she couldn't help but feel badly about what she had done, and the lies she had told.

She hoped Tony would believe her and forgive her, and she hoped she could forgive herself as well. She moved close to him, placing her hands on his waist. He looked at her for a moment, then pulled her close to him and kissed her gently on the forehead.

"I'm sorry for not trusting you, I don't know what's gotten into me lately, but with all the stuff going on with planning the wedding, you quitting your job and trying to redo the patio, I guess I was just stressed out. You've never given me a reason not to trust you, I'm sorry I questioned you, can you forgive me?"

"Of course," she wrapped her arms around him and they held each other tightly until the phone began to ring. At first they both looked at the cordless phone, but then realized it was one of the cell phones.

"I'll get it," he said as he reached for her phone. "Hello? Sure hold on, can I tell her who's calling?" He handed the phone to Riley, "it's Kelsey."

It took a minute for the name to register, Taylor's daughter's name was Kelsey, she was willing to bet that he was the mysterious hang-up caller and now he probably had some woman call and ask for her just in case Tony answered the phone. Riley toyed with the idea of taking the call, but since she was so unsure as to who was on the other end, she decided against it.

"Tell her I'll call her back later," she said as she walked into the other room.

"She'll have to call you back later." She heard Tony tell the caller as she closed the bathroom door. She sat on the carpeted toilet cover and rested her head in her hands. 'What have you gotten yourself into?' She asked herself. She was so lost in thought that time slipped past her, next thing she heard was Tony knocking on the bathroom door.

"Riley, you okay?"

"Uh, sure, fine," was all that came out. She turned on the faucet and splashed cool water on her face before opening the door.

Tony was standing there waiting for her. He looked concerned. "Sure you're okay?"

"Yeah, fine. Just had a bit of a stomachache." She laughed at the thought. A stomachache! That was probably the first true statement she had said to him all day. "Do we have any of those chewy antacids?"

"There in the kitchen cabinet, why don't you go lie down and I'll bring them up to you?"

"Thanks honey," she said as he headed back towards the kitchen. She turned and went upstairs, thinking a nice nap would do her good. As she climbed into bed she could hear Tony opening and closing the kitchen cabinets looking for antacids.

She must have dozed off before Tony came upstairs; she awoke to find the antacid bottle on the nightstand along with a glass of water. She glanced at the clock, almost five already; time to get moving the day was practically gone. She pushed off the quilt that Tony had thrown over her and sat up.

Her stomach was feeling better; the nap was more beneficial than she had thought it would be. She made her way to the bathroom, turned on the faucet, splashed cool water on her face, ran a comb through her hair and brushed her teeth quickly before heading downstairs.

"Tony," she called as she reached the bottom of the steps.

"In here." He was lying on the couch watching a baseball game.

"Who's winning?"

"Couldn't tell you. Feeling better?"

"Yes, much thanks for the water and stuff, it really helped." She sat down next to him, resting her head on his shoulder. "Anyone call?"

"Just my mom, wanted to know what we were doing for dinner. I told her we had plans." He stroked her hair, "you still up for a romantic evening?"

"Most definitely. In fact, I'll start cooking pretty soon, you hungry?"

"A little. I need to run out for a little bit, still have a few errands to run and I didn't want to leave you alone. Now that you're up, I'll go take care of my stuff and I'll be back in about an hour or so." He stood up, walked to the table and grabbed his wallet and keys. Riley was grateful he was acting more like his normal self again.

"See you in a bit," he said as he leaned over and kissed her on the head, then walked out the door. A moment later she heard the engine start and his car pulling out of the drive.

Riley stared at the baseball game on the television for a few more minutes before switching the TV off and going towards the kitchen.

She opened the refrigerator and took out the food she had bought for dinner. Riley had seasoned the swordfish, placed it in the oven to bake, put the vegetables into the steamer and was about the fix the potatoes when the phone rang. Placing the potatoes onto the counter and tossing the oven mitt next to the pan, she ran into the living room to answer it. It was then she realized it was her cell phone again. She hesitated for a moment, then reached over, picked it up and pressed the answer button. "Hello?"

There was a slight hesitation on the other end, then a male voice spoke very softly, "Riley?"

"Yes, who's this?" The voice was so soft she could not recognize the caller, so the next sentence took her off guard.

"Riley, it's me, Taylor." He must have sensed her surprise, "Riley, you there?"

"Yes, I'm here." She was not sure what to say to him. Just hearing his voice sent a strange sensation through her, her body began to tingle with anticipation. "How are you?"

"Fine now that I've heard your voice."

It was almost as if Riley was two separate people, Tony's fiancée' and Taylor's love interest. The second personality emerged and Riley heard herself respond to him, "I'm glad you called. It may sound silly, but I was beginning to miss you."

"Doesn't sound silly to me, I began missing you as soon as you left the parking lot last night."

"You did?" Riley's flirtatious side was emerging in full force now. "How much did you miss me?" she asked coyly.

"A lot. It has been a long time since I have had the desire for anyone the way I desire to be with you."

"Oh? Well then, tell me when you plan to see me again..."

"Are you free tonight?"

Riley's sensible side tried to fight her response, but again her flirtatious personality won over, "not tonight, how's tomorrow night?"

"There's a spot on the boardwalk I'd like to take you to. Meet me at 9:30 on the corner of Atlantic and Ocean Ave. I've got to go now, I'll see you tomorrow."

Riley couldn't help but smile at the thought of seeing him again, "I'll be there," she said as she disconnected the phone. She held the phone to her chest, took a deep breath and said, "I'll definitely be there."

"Definitely be where?"

She jumped. The question took her by surprise, she had not realized she had spoken out loud, more importantly, she had not realized Tony had come home.

"Tony, I didn't hear you come in."

"I gathered that. Who were you talking to?"

"Kim. She wanted to go to the movies tomorrow night, I told her I'd meet her there."

"Oh. Tell her I said hello" was all he said as he walked back into the house. As reality hit her, she scolded herself for being so nonchalant about the situation. She was also angry with herself for getting so wrapped up in talking with Taylor that she did not hear Tony come into the house and out onto the patio where she had been sitting on a lounge chair chatting away. What if he had overheard more than the last part of the conversation? What if he was just testing her by asking her who she was talking to? The questions were running through her mind one on top of another, her thoughts racing so fast her head began to throb. She reached up to rub her temples in an effort to make herself relax. She tried talking to herself, calming words, reassuring herself that if Tony had heard more than the tail end of the conversation he would have been furious, not as laid back as he was.

No, he only heard the last sentence, that's all. 'Relax,' she told herself, 'everything will be okay.' She was still rubbing her temples, when Tony came back out onto the patio.

"Honey, you okay? You look a little flushed."

"No, I'm fine, just came out here to get fresh air while I was talking to Kim, guess I didn't realize it was still so hot out."

"In that case, come back inside and have one of my amazing frozen daiquiris, which will definitely cool you off." He smiled.

Riley was now assured he did not hear anything but the last comment she had made to Taylor before hanging up. She smiled back at him as she stood up and followed him back into the house. The smell of baked fish and steaming vegetables had filled the house. Riley put the potatoes in the oven and began to set the table while Tony mixed up a blender full of frozen strawberries along with his "secret ingredients" as he called them. Even after all this time she still had no idea what he put into his drinks, but whatever the ingredients were, he made the best strawberry daiquiri's she'd ever tasted.

They took their drinks back out to the patio and sat on the double lounge chair, his arm around her, her head resting on his chest. It seemed as if they lay there for hours, neither one of them saying a word, Tony stroking Riley's head softly.

Finally he spoke, "so, what do you think about putting a plant in that corner over there?"

"What?" Riley had drifted off into a state of relaxation, not clearly fixated on anything in particular. "I'm sorry, what was that?"

"I said what do you think about putting a plant in that corner?" He pointed to the far end of the patio.

Riley chuckled, "do you mean on top of the junk that is there now?"

"Very funny, I mean after the place is cleared out and the tile has been laid."

"Tile? What are you talking about?"

"Oh, I found this guy, well, I haven't actually talked with him, but I heard that he was really good at laying outdoor tile, sort of like the Mexican tile, but a little less expensive. Anyway, I was going to call him this week and have him come out and give us an estimate. After all, eventually we are going to entertain here at the house and it would be nice to have a patio for people to sit on."

"You're right. That sounds good, why don't you call him and have him come out over the weekend."

"Consider it done. Now, let's eat!"

They headed back inside to the enticing aroma of dinner. The daiquiri relaxed Riley more than she had realized. Halfway through dinner exhaustion overtook her. "I guess our romantic evening is going to be an early one, huh?" Tony said.

"I guess so," Riley replied yawning as she cleared the dishes from the table. "I'm not sure why the drink affected me so much, but if you don't mind doing the dishes, I'm going to head upstairs to sleep."

Smiling, he leaned over to kiss her, whispering, "goodnight sleepyhead, I'll be up in a little bit."

Chapter 6

Riley undressed quickly, bundling herself under the covers as she climbed into bed. Sleep overtook her as soon as her head hit the pillow. The next thing Riley knew something was leaning on her arm. She tried to wiggle free of the pressure in her sleep, but was not successful and was forced to open her eyes. She found Tony leaning on his elbow, his hand holding her shoulder, gently pushing her back and forth.

"What are you doing?" She asked.

"Maybe I should be asking you what you are doing. Who's Taylor?"

The sleep cleared quickly from Riley's eyes as she sat straight up in bed. "What?"

"You've been moaning about someone named Taylor for the last half hour, so who is he?"

By the look in Tony's eyes she could tell he was more than a little annoyed, she decided to take the humor approach, simply saying, "oh, don't get so worked up, I can't help it if my mind wanders and James Taylor enters my dreams. It's not like he's going to show up and steal me away to a desert island." She laughed at her own joke. Tony, on the other hand, did not look amused. She kissed him gently on the lips as she laid down, curling up under the covers.

"Goodnight," she said as she closed her eyes, trying to calm her heartbeat and hoping Tony would think she was sleeping. It took a moment, but Riley then heard him lie back down, followed moments later by his snoring. She relaxed a little, and then scolded herself for saying Taylor's name out loud and in her sleep no less. Things were not going well. Her mind began to race; thoughts of Taylor, thoughts of Tony, the lies she had told, and the wedding all cluttered her mind. Suddenly, her head began to pound. Then her heart began to pound faster, it was becoming harder to breathe as panic set in.

What was she doing? Dreaming about one man, while in bed with the man she was going to marry, not to mention that she had a date with the man in her dreams the next night, while her finance' was working. It was overwhelming her; she knew things were not going to get any better unless she made some changes. But what? How to handle difficult situations was Riley's strong point. She was not one to make hasty decisions and therefore in this situation where an outsider would say to just forget about Taylor and get on with life with Tony, Riley was unable to.

She felt that everything happened for a reason and she needed to see this thing out in order to find out the reason Taylor was brought into her life. It may sound stupid to an outsider, but to Riley it seemed the natural thing to do, see it through, whatever the consequences may be. Her heartbeat began to slow; her breathing became more relaxed as she came to the conclusion that whatever was to be, will be. She would have to see it through and hope that some good would come of it. With that thought, she drifted off to sleep, dreaming sweet dreams of Taylor.

Chapter 7

The next morning came quickly. As she rolled over, Riley was thankful she had taken some time off from work to focus on her personal life. Although Tony's new habit of getting up and being long gone before she awoke was beginning to annoy her. 'This is getting boring, real quick,' she thought as she began to rethink her decision to move in with Tony. Maybe she needed some space to think this thing through. It was hard on her, but she had to be fair and admit to herself that it was probably very frustrating to Tony, not knowing what was going on with her. Riley knew if things were the other way around, she would be very annoyed already and would not put up with the secretiveness for very long. She got up and dressed quickly, then headed downstairs to grab something to eat. As she headed out the door with a pop-tart in her hand, something caught her eye. The morning paper. As if by reflex, she grabbed it and walked out the door.

Riley had her list of things to do lying on the seat next to her. Suddenly, the list became second priority as she flipped to the real estate section of the paper. It wouldn't hurt to look at an apartment or two, she thought. Tony would never know and if things calm down, then it wouldn't matter anyway. On the other hand, it would be best if she knew what was out there, just in case she needed to move.

She began driving up the main highway, towards the beach. Riley had always loved the beach. Growing up in Manalapan with her parents, her bedroom balcony overlooked the ocean, and she spent countless hours sitting on the balcony, reading with the wind blowing on her face, the smell of the sea air. Without realizing where she was going, Riley managed to drive as if on autopilot, to her family home. From the road, it was monstrous, although not as huge as it had seemed when she was little.

She pulled into the drive of the beachfront mansion for the first time since her parents' death. After the night of the phone call, Riley stayed in her room for a while, sinking into a deep depression. It took strong medications and hours of therapy for her to be able to cope with the loss. Finally, after Maria left, she decided that the best thing for her to do was lock up the house and move into an apartment in town to try and regain some semblance of a normal life. It was shortly after that move, she met Tony.

Riley froze as a chill ran through her. Her life had been such a whirlwind since her parents' death that she had not stopped to "smell the flowers" as her mother would have said. "You have to stop and smell the flowers or life will pass you by quicker than you can bat an eye" was her mother's favorite saying. Her mother always told her to slow down and enjoy her life, because if she didn't, by the time she realized what she had missed, it would be too late. Maybe mom was right, Riley thought. Maybe my life has been going by too fast and I just didn't want to slow it down because I'm afraid of what I might see. Emotions and thoughts jumbled Riley's mind, fear, anxiety, excitement, and a terrible sense of sadness.

Uncontrollably, she began to sob, like a child who was lost in the middle of a store. All Riley longed for at this very moment was a few precious minutes with her parents. "Oh Lord, just let me have them back for a little while longer, just one more hug, one more I love you" she sobbed through her tears. Resting her head on the steering wheel, Riley let the tears flow from her, pictures of her parents flashed through her mind, her desire to be with them one more time almost unbearable, inside she knew that this was the release she had held back for so long, now it was time to let go. Riley cried for almost an hour. When she was done, she wiped the tears from her swollen eyes and looked at herself in the rearview mirror.

Taking a deep breath, she told herself that it was time to go back and face her demons; this was something she needed to do in order to move forward with her life. She pressed the accelerator and the car moved toward the gate. She put her key in the gate box, turned it slowly and listened to the whine of the gate as she prepared to confront her past for the first time in over a year.

Riley pulled the car to the top of the circular drive, parking in front of the steps to the front door. Although this was the house she was born in and had grown up in, it seemed very unfamiliar to her at this moment. A stranger in her own home. She got out of the car; the door seemed to make a thunderous sound as it closed in the silence of the estate grounds. She fumbled in her pockets for the keychain with the house keys on it. It took only a moment and she was standing in front of the large double doors at the top of the stairs. At first the cleanliness of the doors surprised her, then Riley remembered that Sam, the caretaker had stayed on to take care of the house and grounds. He lived in a cottage on the back part of the property, making the three mile trip to the main house by golf cart each day. Sam was a quiet old man who had been taking care of the Matthews' estate long before Riley had been born, and who would probably live out his last days here as well. The key turned in the lock, and the front door opened, the foyer in its grand elegance displayed. Riley entered slowly, she gasped for breath, almost panicking until she realized that she had been holding her breath as she entered the house. Talking to herself, she said, "just keep breathing as you walk and you'll be fine."

It took only a few minutes and Riley was overcome with a sense of warmth and comfort as she walked through the house. She began to relax a bit, as scenes from her childhood flashed through her mind. Standing in the doorway to the small playroom off the kitchen, Riley could hear her mother's voice telling her to clean up before dinner, to put her toys away.

Riley had not played in the room for many years before her parents had died, and had asked her mother many times why she did not get rid of the toys and make the room into something more useful. Mrs. Matthews would smile every time Riley asked, and then she would simply say, "this room is more useful than you think. Every time I go in here, I can close my eyes and see you dancing, playing and smiling as my beautiful little girl. The memories of your childhood are more special to me than you can imagine. For they are all I have because now my little girl is all grown up and making new memories as a young lady." There were many times Riley would ask her mother that very same question just to hear the answer, to hear the pride in her mother's voice when she spoke about her little girl.

"Looks the same, doesn't it?" Riley was so caught up in the memories, that she had not heard Sam walk up next to her. He must have sensed her surprise. "I'm sorry, Riley, I hadn't meant to startle you."

"No, it's all right. I was a bit caught up in my thoughts."

"Thoughts of your mother, I presume?"

Riley looked at Sam, his eyes surrounded by deep lines. He was a kind old man, the only grandfather figure Riley had ever known.

Riley could remember the times she spent playing her own version of hide and seek with him while he tried to trim the hedges. She would find a spot behind a bush that needed trimming and would jump out when he walked by. Most of the time he seemed to be scared, but by the time Riley was 8 or 9, she realized that he always knew where she was and that his gasp was more for her sake than real.

"Riley?"

"I'm sorry Sam. It's just that it seems so overwhelming to be back here."

"I must admit I was surprised when I saw the car out front. I mean, I did expect you to return to your home someday, just not today."

She looked at him, puzzled. "Why not today?"

"Riley, don't tell me you forgot."

She thought for a moment, then it hit her like a ton of bricks. Her parents' anniversary was today. Maybe that is why she had been so out of sorts these past few days. Her mind was trying to remember and she had been blocking it out. "I guess I knew, but didn't want to think about it."

"These things happen for a reason. Maybe it was time for you to come home; after all, it has been a long time."

"You're right, maybe it's time. I have a lot going on right now and I guess I have gotten to a point where I couldn't move forward without dealing with the past. So here I am."

"So here you are. I think if you're planning to take on the past and move onto the future, you'd better have a good meal first. I was just about to make some lunch, how about joining me for some peanut butter and banana sandwiches?"

Riley couldn't help but laugh out loud. "Don't tell me you still eat that?" She remembered the summer days when she would make peanut butter and banana sandwiches for the two of them and they would sit under the big melaluca tree staring at the clouds, drinking lemonade.

"I never stopped eating them, although I always hoped that one day my favorite lunch date would come back to eat with me again."

"Well, looks like today's your lucky day!" As he reached out his hand, he smiled, a warm caring smile, with a kindness and sincerity she had not felt in a long time. She slipped her hand into his and they headed off towards the kitchen.

Time flew by quickly as they reminisced about her parents and her childhood. For Riley it was a cleansing experience. She felt as though by talking with Sam she was able to free herself from the guilt and fear she had unknowingly carried around for so long. Riley knew that Sam understood why she was hurting, losing her parents as a teenager, being forced to raise herself, longing for the stability of a family that was no longer there, it was not easy on her. Until this moment, she had not realized how difficult and alone she had felt.

Sam shared his feelings with her, the guilt and the loneliness he too had felt after he lost not only her parents, but his wife as well within the same year. Her parents had been the children he and his wife never had. He had taken care of the grounds while Adele took care of the cooking. Together they kept the Matthews household running smoothly, excellent help one might say, but they were more than help, they were family, and Sam was the only person left who could genuinely understand her.

They talked for hours, walking through the house sharing memories. Day turned into night as the sun began to set over the ocean. They walked out onto the balcony, overlooking the moonlit ocean. "I didn't realize how much I missed being here until now," she said.

"There's nothing stopping you from coming home, Riley."

"I don't know Sam, I mean, yes Tony and I are having some problems, actually, I'm having problems and Tony is just there; but, I don't know what would happen if I moved back here. I don't feel comfortable living here with Tony."

"So don't live here with Tony. Come home, live by yourself for a while, date Tony or whoever you want to date..."

Riley looked at Sam, the twinkle in his eye told her that even though she had told him about Tony, he knew that there was more to the story. "How did you know?"

"Riley Matthews I've known you since before the day you were born, I may seem to be just a feeble-minded old man, but in reality, I'm a pretty smart guy. I know there is more to the story, you haven't found the happiness you were looking for with Tony and my guess would be that you hadn't realized that until you met someone else. Now you're confused as to what to do, and that confusion has led you home."

She smiled, "I couldn't have said it better myself. Thank you for understanding."

"You're quite welcome. So, are you going to come home? This house has been awfully empty without you."

Glancing at her watch she said, "I'll think about it. Right now I'd better go." As the words came out of her mouth she realized it was almost 9:30, her meeting time with Taylor. She kissed Sam gently on the cheek as he walked her to her car. "I'll be back soon, I promise."

"Sooner than you may think," he said as he stood in the doorway watching Riley drive off towards the gate.

Chapter 8

Riley drove along Ocean Avenue towards Atlantic Boulevard. Traffic was light and the drive took less time than she had anticipated. She reached the traffic light at the intersection of Atlantic and Ocean. "Now where?" she asked herself. To the left was the beach, to the right a condominium and then she saw it, across the street behind a small cafe, was a parking lot. It had only a half a dozen parking spots so it was easy for Riley to notice Taylor's truck. She turned into the lot and parked a few spots over. He got out of his truck and was standing at her door before she could turn the engine off.

"I'm glad you made it, I was beginning to think you weren't coming."

"Funny, Taylor, I've met you every time you've asked me to, why would you think that I wasn't coming this time?" Her first impression was that something was wrong, they had met several times already and this time he seemed a bit off, she couldn't quite put her finger on it, but there was something different about him.

He glanced at his watch, "it's past 9:30."

She checked her watch against his, sure enough; Riley's watch had stopped at 9:15. "Sorry, I was in the middle of something when I realized I was supposed to meet you. I guess I hadn't noticed that my watch had stopped."

"Whatever. Let's take a walk along the beach." He took her hand as if to lead her across the street. Not knowing why, she fought the urge to pull her hand away from him. Maybe she was still in a whirlwind from spending the day with Sam at the house, or maybe it was because she felt that she was being unfaithful to Tony, whatever it was it was making her uncomfortable and she did not like that one bit.

She came out here to meet Taylor because she had enjoyed talking with him the last few times they had been together, now something was telling her to run, to get far away from him. He did not seem to notice her cringing as they walked across the street, his hand holding hers tightly.

They walked over the sand, she barely spoke as he began to ramble on about how glad he was she had come to meet him, saying that he was nervous and afraid she wasn't going to be here and even more so when 9:30 came and went and she still hadn't arrived.

Riley was half listening to his babbling, her gut instinct was still telling her to go home, that there was something wrong with Taylor, she couldn't put her finger on it, so to speak, but there was something terribly wrong with this situation. "Riley? Are you going to take off your shoes, or are you planning to let them get soaked by the waves?"

"Huh?" She looked down just as the water hit her feet. Turning, she looked at the stark beach behind them, they had walked over 40 feet to the ocean and she had not noticed until the cold water hit her feet and sent a shiver through her spine. "I guess it's too late now."

"Guess so."

They continued to walk along the water, waves splashing their feet. The silence between them was strange. There was no reason for the silence and yet it seemed as if neither one of them had anything to say.

Finally, he broke the silence, "Riley, you are a beautiful woman, and I'm very fortunate to have you in my life." His statement took her by surprise, leaving her fumbling for a response. Before she could open her mouth to speak, he leaned over and kissed her. "I've wanted to do that since the last time I saw you."

"Taylor, I think we should take things slowly. You and Jeni just split up, and I have a situation of my own to work on."

"Jeni and I are through. She and Kelsey are gone, there's nothing more to that relationship. And you and Tony will be done soon, once you tell him that you and I are seeing each other, I'm pretty sure he'll understand that you two won't be getting married."

The sharpness of his words stunned Riley. Who was he to make a decision like that for her? What did he mean they were gone? His nonchalant attitude towards Jeni bothered her. As much as he may dislike her right now, he was still married to her and she was the mother of his child. How could he be so cold? Who was this man? It was almost as if the Taylor she had met a few weeks before was now gone and this horrid man had taken over his body. Riley now felt extremely uncomfortable with him and wanted to leave.

She turned to him, "Taylor, I'm sorry; I think this was a bad idea, I'm going to go home." With that, she turned her back to him and began to walk towards the street.

He followed her, within two steps he was walking side by side with her, trying desperately to talk to her. "Riley, please listen to me, I may have been a bit abrupt tonight, but that is only because I've had a really bad day and I didn't have time to clear my head. I'm really sorry; I should never have taken it out on you."

Riley keep walking, she had heard what he said, but had no desire to be anywhere near a man who could switch personalities so quickly. Apparently, Taylor was not one to take no for an answer, as he grabbed her arm and spun her around so she was facing him. "Riley, I'm talking to you," he yelled at her.

She looked him straight in the eyes, not knowing where the force was coming from. "Let go of my arm," she said, keeping her eyes focused on his. "Taylor, you have two seconds to let go of me or I will scream so loudly people six blocks away will hear me. I'm not sure what your problem is, but at this point I don't care. Now, I repeat. Let...go...of...my...arm."

Her firmness startled him enough to release his grip on her arm. She glanced down and saw the color fill in the palm print that he had left on her arm. Without saying a word, she turned and continued to walk to the street. She never looked back. She had not noticed that she had been holding her breath the entire time. Finally gasping for air she closed and locked her car door.

It was after 11:30 when Riley turned onto Oak Ridge Road. She was surprised to see Tony's car was in the driveway, the porch light on. She released a sigh guessing his shift had ended early, and he was now probably waiting for her, no doubt worried, she had been gone all day, had not left a note and he would have no idea where she was. On top of that, she had left her cell phone lying on the floor of the car, she had not noticed the battery light was off; the phone was out of service. She pulled into the driveway and parked the car, taking a deep breath, she decided this was the moment of truth, she had to tell Tony what was going on, being honest with him was the right thing to do.

She hesitated as she got out of the car. This was going to be more difficult that she had thought. She loved Tony, or at least she thought she did. So many things had changed in such a short period of time, she no longer could be sure of her own feelings. She walked towards the front door, fumbling for her keys, and then realizing she was so out of sorts that she had left them in the ignition. She turned to walk back to the car when the door opened. "Not planning on coming home?"

The tone of his voice told her he was not in a pleasant mood. "Tony, I'm really sorry." She stopped herself before the whole story came out. "Look, I left my keys in the car, I'm going to get them and then I'll be in. I need to talk to you."

"I'm glad to hear it. I have a few things I want to say to you too."

She walked to the car, her hands trembling. This was not going to be a good night. Whatever she and Tony had to say to each other, none of it would leave them in a happy place. As she took the keys from the ignition, second thoughts crossed her mind; she could just as easily drive off, never turning back. Reality hit her quickly and the thoughts of running off into the night vanished as she turned and walked into the house.

Tony was sitting at the kitchen table when she walked in. "Pull up a chair."

Riley put her bag down on the couch and joined Tony at the table, sitting across from him. She didn't know what to say, starting this conversation was more difficult than she thought.

Tony, however, did not have that problem. "Riley, I think we have a problem. There are apparently things going on with you that you don't want to tell me about. Whatever they are is irrelevant at this point, the relevant part is that you couldn't talk to me and that's a big problem for me. Communication is the basis of any relationship and obviously we don't have open communication."

"Tony, I'm sorry, I don't know what to say. You're right, things have been going on with me, and it's not that I don't want to discuss them with you, I really do. It's just that things have been happening so fast lately, I don't know if I'm coming or going anymore."

"So you figured if you just ignore me and my feelings everything would be alright?"

"No, nothing like that. I guess everything just spiraled and by the time I turned around... well, here we are."

"Okay, so what you're saying is that you just need to slow down and then you can tell me what's going on?"

Riley looked at him. He looked hurt and hopeful in the same moment. As if he was hoping she would tell him what was happening so he could make it okay and they could get on with their lives. She wished it was that easy. She prayed for the strength to tell him she couldn't marry him, not now anyway, while things were still so hectic in her life. She needed to be by herself to work things through. 'Be strong,' she told herself as she gripped herself to speak, say the words that would forever change their relationship. "Tony, a lot has happened in the past few weeks. I guess the only way to explain it is to start at the beginning. I know it's not something you're going to want to hear, but at this point I think I owe you the truth."

Acting as though he was a child bracing himself for the worst, he entwined his fingers and took a deep breath. "That's fair enough, go ahead."

"Well, a few weeks back I met someone and things began to change. I know now that it had nothing to do with him directly, it was more that he made me realize there was something incomplete about my life. I talked with him a few times, the newness was refreshing, but then he got really weird and I bolted. Tony, I'm not going to lie to you, I kissed him, but it didn't mean anything. He was just there. Anyway, the whole situation had gotten me so confused that I ended up back at the house on the beach. I spent today there with Sam, talking and basically I came to the conclusion that right now I have too much unsettled business in my life, too much to be able to make a commitment to anyone and that's not fair to you."

He stared at her; as if he was unable to put into words the hurt and devastation he was feeling. Although he had said it, Riley knew in his heart, Tony had never actually thought she was out with another man. She figured he had thought planning the wedding without her mother was what was causing her odd behavior. As she was almost certain the thought of her leaving him had never entered the picture, she did her best to fight back the tears as he spoke. "Riley, are you saying you want to move out? If it's space you need, I understand, but I can't understand you wanting to break things off all together." She tried to maintain her composure. "I know it seems sudden and maybe a little extreme, but right now I can't see things clearly and I just want to be by myself to figure it all out."

"I hear what you're saying, but we don't have to split up, do we? I mean, can't you just go wherever it is you want or need to go and then when everything is straightened out; we can get on with the wedding and our lives. Riley, in my wildest dreams I never thought this was about us breaking up. I thought maybe things were tough on you, planning a wedding by yourself, bringing up memories of your mom and stuff like that."

"Maybe that's part of it, but I can't say for sure. I just know that I feel as if I need to get out of here and then maybe I can get a hold of my life again. It's as if things have moved so fast in the past few years, I never took the time to get to know myself and therefore no one else can know who I am."

"Where are you planning to go? Is this guy part of your plan?"

"No. Like I said, he was just there, no one important to me. In fact, the last time I saw him I told him I had nothing left to say to him and that I didn't want him to contact me again. I really don't know what my plan is. I intend to move back to my parent's house and just let things happen. It may sound horrible, but I have a lot of money that I haven't done a thing with. I think now would be a really good time for me to take a cruise or something. I deserve to relax a bit and that's what I'm going to do."

"Well, I see there's nothing I can do about changing your mind, so I guess I have to ask you one more question."

"What's that?"

"If you're not sure you want to spend your life with me, then I think it is only right that you return the engagement ring."

There, it was out. He had asked for the ring back. Riley had not thought about the ring since he had put it on her hand. It seemed to become a part of her, and now he wanted that part back. There was nothing she could say, he was right, if she was so unsure then there was no reason for him to hang onto a dream that may never become a reality. She reached down and slowly took the diamond off her finger. As she handed it to him the consequences of her actions became more real than they had been, it was over, the feelings she thought she had for him disappeared as he took the ring and tossed it into the candy dish on the counter.

"Oh well, guess that's all folks," he said as he grabbed his keys from the coffee table and walked out the front door.

Chapter 9

It was after one in the morning when Tony had walked out. Riley knew him well enough to know he went to one of the local bars to hang out. She called a couple of the places he would most likely have gone to just to make sure he was okay. She found him at Smiley's, drinking like a fish according to the hostess that answered the phone. Riley asked her to keep an eye on him when he left, and even though she assured Riley she would, Riley knew better; people in bars paid no attention to how drunk someone was when they left, only how good the tip was they left behind. Riley just hoped that he was there with friends and someone would stop him from driving drunk. She thought about packing and leaving tonight, but where would she go? As she thought more about it, she figured that she would just go back to the estate and live there for a while, after all, it was hers now. The only problem was that by the time she packed and got out there it would be close to three or four in the morning and since Sam would not expect anyone to be there, it would definitely scare him. Her best bet would be to get some sleep and pack in the morning, if she timed it right she would be in her new home by lunchtime. She also figured that Tony would spend the night at one of his buddies' apartments and not get back here until mid-afternoon, so running into him was not a likely possibility. She locked up the house, turned off the lights, changed into her pj's and tucked herself in for the last time in this house. The alarm went off at seven thirty as it did every morning. Riley reached over for Tony and then pulled her arm back as the previous night's events floated back through her mind. She lay in bed for a moment staring at the ceiling fan spin, faster and faster, just like her life, spinning out of control, her mind was lost in the spinning fan. Finally, she blinked and turned away. She pushed back the covers and got out of bed. Okay, this is what you wanted, let's do it, she said to herself, time to pack. She pulled off her pj's, tossed on a pair of shorts and a T-shirt, pulled her hair back into a ponytail and was ready to go. Opening the closet, she began to toss her clothes onto the bed, hangers and all. She realized as she was packing that she had not brought anything more than the basics. Her old apartment had been furnished, so when she moved in with Tony, it was clothes and knickknacks that came with her. Even though the breakup was a bit saddening, the move would not be difficult at all. Within a half-hour's time her closet and drawers were empty and she was carrying her things out to the car. She piled everything into the trunk, went back for a few miscellaneous items and a can of soda and she was ready to leave by nine o'clock.

She wasn't sure what to do next since Tony wasn't home. She really hadn't expected him to be, but she felt uncomfortable leaving things the way they were. She was sure he did not come home simply because he thought she would still be here and he was giving her time to get her things together and go. There was nothing more she could do, she started to write a note, but for the first time in a long time, she had nothing to say. She forced herself to write something simple, "hopefully, we can talk later" was how she left it. She locked the door, closed the trunk and passenger door and got in the car. She paused for only a moment, reminding herself this was the best thing for everyone involved especially her. She stated the ignition and turned up the radio as she drove back towards the main road, she did not see the truck sitting across the street in the driveway of the only house on the block for sale.

The driver watched her pull away, in fact the driver had been watching her since the night before, when she came back all flustered and hurried. It was a little strange when the man left last night, and then this morning when the girl packed what seemed to be everything she owned into her car, the driver knew something was amiss in the happy household. One guess as to what had happened, an argument of some sorts had taken place and while the man was out blowing off steam, the girl was moving out on him. Not knowing where the girl was going, the driver could only speculate the worst case scenario and this time, things were going to be different. This time the driver would win out, not the girl. The truck backed out of the driveway and turned towards the main road, prepared to follow the girl wherever she was going, keeping her in sight was very important if things were going to happen as the driver planned.

The truck followed Riley along the coast road heading north towards the more affluent homes. She slowed down and pulled up in front of a mansion on the water. The driver slowed and pulled off into the brush on the opposite side of the road, what was the girl doing here?

Riley pulled out the remote for the gate and clicked it once. The gate did not whine as much this time as it had the first time she opened it, in fact just being here made her feel more at ease, more comfortable than she had felt in the past few weeks. She drove up the main drive, this time turning towards the right instead of continuing on the circular drive. As she parked her car in front of the garage door, she remembered her parents' cars were still inside; she had never done anything with them after their deaths. A slight chill ran through her as she got out of the car. She felt as if she was being watched, as if eyes were following her every move. She told herself she was being ridiculous, Sam was probably around somewhere and it was his presence she felt. As she punched the code into the keypad on the side of the garage door, Sam appeared. "Well, I'm glad to see you made it home."

She hugged him, "I'm glad to be home, Sam."

The garage door opened revealing her parents' cars, her mother's Mercedes convertible and her father's two corvettes. The cars shined like they were brand new. "You've been taking care of them," she said, looking at Sam. It was obvious someone had been washing and waxing the cars over the past few years, and who better to do that than the man who loved her parents as much as she did.

"It gave me a way to remember fun times with your parents. Your dad and I used to wash the cars together and then your mom would always come out with drinks for us. Somehow it always turned into a water fight; by the time we were done we had more water on us than the cars did."

She smiled at the memory, she could almost hear her mother's shrieks as her father sprayed her with the hose or threw a soapy sponge at her. They were truly in love and even though she did not physically have them anymore, the one thing she was grateful for was that they had died together, loving each other until the end.

"Sam, thank you for being here, it means a lot to me."

"Riley, this has been my home for over 25 years, you are the only family I have left and I will always be here for you. Now, let's get your things inside."

They opened the trunk and began to unload her clothing, walking through the garage, Sam headed towards her old bedroom. She followed him in a daze, as if being led by the Pied Piper. He stopped in front of her bedroom door, stepping aside to let her go in front of him. She paused in front of the door, then slowly reached out to the doorknob and turned it. The door swung open, she stood in the doorway mesmerized by what she saw.

The room looked exactly as it had the last time she had slept in it, her hunter green comforter, the sun blazing through the cream colored curtains she and her mother had hung on her twelfth birthday. Her mind flashed back to that day, she had firmly decided she was too grown up for the pastel pink flowers that had covered the walls and the matching pink curtains on the windows. Her mother smiled and agreed that she was old enough to know what she liked and disliked, so if she didn't like the way her bedroom was decorated, it was time for a change. Riley was allowed to skip school for the day and they went on a shopping outing, she had picked out the curtains, comforter and towels all by herself. Hunter green and cream, she found the color combination rather soothing and appealing. They spent the entire day hanging curtains and changing sheets and towels. Her mother had even suggested painting a border in the bathroom, roses and leaves to match her color scheme. Her mother hand painted the border while Riley handled cleaning the brushes and providing paint. Her father coming home followed by a furniture truck full of adult furniture for her topped off the night. They moved her old furniture up into the attic and replaced it with handcrafted, wood dressers, chests and a four-poster bed. Nothing had come close to topping that day in all of Riley's years since. It was almost as if that was the day she could pinpoint as the day she became an adult. She took a deep breath and walked into the room. Sam followed her lead and placed her clothes on the chair in the corner. Riley began opening the curtains in to allow the sun to flow through the room. She loved the fact that her room had overlooked both the front grounds and the beach in back of the house. She stopped briefly at the balcony door that overlooked the front grounds and the main road. Something caught her eye. Parked across the street was a dark sport utility truck, with a person in it. From the distance Riley could not make out the figure well enough to determine if it was a man or a woman, but whoever it was, they were definitely watching the house. She quickly closed the curtains and moved away form the doors. Unsure as to why someone would be watching the house, she decided it was probably best if she kept her guard up. She turned back to Sam, but he was gone.

"Sam?" That's odd, she thought, where is he?

A moment later her question was answered as he walked back into the room with the rest of her clothes over his arms. "That's all of it. It's official, you're moved in."

"Thanks, I really appreciate the help. I think I'm going to lie down for a while. Pathetic, huh? The day isn't even half over and I'm exhausted already."

He laughed. "Riley, you've been through a lot in the past few weeks. Take some time to rest, let your body and mind catch up to each other. I've got some yard work to do, so I'll let you get settled. If you need anything, just call."

"Thank you."

Sam smiled as he turned and left the room, closing the door behind him. Riley was alone. It seemed odd at first, being alone in such an enormous house. When she was little there were always people around, but now, only Sam remained and he didn't even live in the house itself. It was going to be strange sleeping in a mansion all alone. Just then a thought crossed Riley's mind. She didn't have to sleep here all alone. Kim would love to stay here with her. In fact, she began to scold herself for not keeping in touch with Kim lately. The events of the past few weeks had been so chaotic that she had almost forgotten her best friend. Not a nice thing, Riley, she said to herself. Fortunately, things like this could be rectified. She picked up the phone and dialed Kim's number. Actually, she hit the speed dial button on her old phone, after all, she and Kim had been friends forever it seemed. When they were younger they played for hours at a time in the big old house, hide and seek obviously their favorite game. The phone rang three times before Kim answered.

"Hello?"

"Hey, it's me. How are you?"

"Riley? Where have you been? I was beginning to worry about you."

"Sorry, I didn't mean to worry you. Things have been crazy lately and I've made a few changes in my life."

"What are you talking about?"

"Kim, I moved back to the estate."

There was silence on the other end of the phone. "Kim? you there?"

"Yes, I'm here. What's going on? Are you alright?"

"Everything is okay, I guess. Tony and I split up. There have been things going on that I haven't told you about, and I really don't want to talk about it on the phone. There's a reason I called."

"What's the reason?"

Riley wandered over to the front balcony and glanced out through the side of the curtains, the black sport utility was still parked across the street, the driver still watching the house. "Well, I was thinking, I know your parents wouldn't mind having the house to themselves, so I was thinking maybe you'd want to stay here with me for a while."

Kim gasped out loud. Riley could tell that Kim's face was not large enough for the grin she had at this very moment. From the time Kim and Riley were little girls, they had talked about getting a place of their own, being adults together. Kim had always joked, saying that they could live in the mansion and since it was so large her parents would never know they were there. Riley knew it was Kim's dream to live in an oceanfront estate. She had been raised in the middle-class section of town, her house was small and quaint, nothing like the dream home she told Riley she wanted to live in.

"Kim, what do you think? You up to living the high life on the beach?"

"Riley, you know my answer! When do we move?"

"We'll, I'm here already, so whenever you get here, you get here."

"I'm packing as we speak, I'll see you in a little while."

Riley laughed as she hung up the phone. She was glad Kim had said yes to the idea of them living in the house. As much as she felt at home in the house, it seemed so big and empty right now, and with the sport utility parked out front, she felt better knowing that there would be someone else in the house with her.

Unpacking took more time than packing had taken. Probably because every time Riley opened a drawer she found an old outfit or trinket that she had left behind and the memories were flowing like a waterfall. Time passed quickly as Riley finally stopped puttering around with every memento she stumbled onto. She put her clothes and toiletries away and then decided to jump into a quick shower. She turned on the water and went to grab some fresh clothes from the dresser, passing the front balcony doors; she couldn't help but glance outside. The truck was still parked in the same place, the driver sitting patiently inside. Riley checked the locks and went back to the bathroom. "You're worrying yourself over nothing," she said out loud as she climbed into the shower stall.

The water was refreshing and she closed her eyes as it splashed on her face. Time to relax she told herself, this is my time to heal. She was standing in the bathroom wearing her robe and a towel on her head when she heard the door to the bedroom open. That's odd, no one should be in the house, and Sam would certainly not open her bedroom door without calling her name first. She began to panic, but that did not last long as she heard Kim's voice calling her name a moment later.

"Riley? You here?"

"In here," she called back.

Kim appeared in the doorway to the bathroom carrying what seemed to be everything she owned in two big duffel bags.

"Packing light I see," Riley joked.

"Never know what a girl might need living the posh lifestyle we'll be living."

Riley couldn't help but laugh. "Okay, Ms. Posh Lifestyle, let's get you settled in so I can finish drying my hair."

"I'm following you."

They walked out of Riley's bedroom and into the hallway.

"Okay, what's your pleasure?" Riley played tour guide moving her hands as she spoke. "To the left we have the presidential suite, complete with a view of the ocean, or if you prefer overlooking the landscape in front of the estate, to the right we have the blue room. So, what'll it be?"

Kim giggled, "I think I'll take the presidential suite this week and the blue room next week," she said as she opened the door to the guest room Riley had dubbed the presidential suite and preceded to put her bags on the bed. "This one will do just fine."

With that both girls laughed out loud.

Kim turned to Riley, looking serious, she said, "are you going to tell me what's going on? Or am I going to have to guess?"

Riley sat down on the bed, Kim sat next to her. "Kim, I don't know how to explain what has happened recently. I just know that right now I need time to gather my thoughts and regroup."

"Can you at least tell me what triggered this whole thing? Did Tony do something?"

"No, Tony didn't do anything wrong, I did. Oh well, I guess you're going to hear the story sooner or later, so I'll tell you, but you have to promise not to be judgmental about any of it. Okay?"

"Fair enough, but I have one question before you start."

"Shoot."

"Can we talk over Oreos and milk? I'm feeling like this is going to be a conversation that definitely needs junk food."

Riley couldn't help but smile, Kim knew her too well, this was definitely an Oreo moment. "To the kitchen we go, Oreos here we come." Kim was only a step behind as they skipped down the hall towards the stairs. Riley was halfway down the stairs when she stopped so suddenly Kim crashed into her almost tossing her down the stairs head first.

"Riley, what is it?"

"Kim, did you leave the front door open when you came in?"

"No, I came in through the garage door. Sam was out there, he let me in. Why?"

"Look." Riley pointed at the front door. The door stood wide open, the front stoop in plain view.

"Oh, maybe Sam's in the house. He's getting older and maybe he's not as quick as he was, it's possible he came in and just didn't close the door." Riley continued to stare at the open front door.

"Riley, hey don't worry about it. It's nothing, just a door that was accidentally left open. Come on, let's get us some Oreos." Kim grabbed Riley's shirtsleeve and lead her down the rest of the stairs. She walked over and closed the door, throwing the deadbolt into place. "There, all fixed. Now I want to hear the juicy gossip that's been going on." Kim walked off towards the kitchen. Riley following her, every few steps glancing back at the front door. Kim piled the Oreos high onto a plate and filled two glasses with milk. Kim placed one glass in front of Riley along with the plate of cookies, and they sat down at the table. "Okay, spill it. I want to hear the whole sordid story."

At first it was hard for Riley to talk, her thoughts were jumbled and more importantly, she was ashamed of what had happened between herself and Taylor. She started off slowly, but then the words began to spill out of her like water flowing from atop a mountain waterfall. She told Kim about how she and Taylor met secretly and talked for hours, their intimate encounters and ultimately his mood swings that scared her to the point where she wanted nothing more to do with him. Then she told her about how she wasn't sure of what was going to happen with Tony, she loved him, but if she could be swayed so easily by Taylor who knows what else could happen. She was afraid that she couldn't be trusted with a commitment to one person. Finally, Riley heard herself talking about the weird occurrences that had happened since she had met Taylor, the phone call telling her to stay away from him and the sport utility truck that had been following her for who knows how long and was now parked outside of the house.

Apparently the final remark was enough to elicit a response from Kim, "parked outside of this house?"

"That's what I said."

Kim stood up and walked to the front room, she pulled back the curtains and from where she stood could make out the truck and a person sitting in the driver's seat right in front of the house, just as Riley had said. "Who do you think it is?"

"I have no idea. Ever since I met Taylor, things in my life have been less than predictable and, therefore, I stopped trying to guess what's happening and what could happen next."

Kim's eyes grew wide, "what do you mean, what could happen next? Do you think that whoever is in that truck is here to harm you?'

"Kim, I really don't know, but the fact that there is someone sitting in front of a house that has been unoccupied for over a year is strange in and of itself. Now mix that with fact that I moved back in today, and things become even odder."

"You think someone is stalking you, don't you?" The panic in Kim's voice was clear, "Riley, call the police!" she said in a shaky voice as she handed her the receiver from the kitchen phone.

"Kim, I'm not going to call the police. What would I tell them? I have no idea as to why that truck is in front of my home and until I do, I'm not going to go overboard with panic." Riley returned the receiver to the hook and sat back down with her milk and cookies. "Look, I told you what was going on because you're my best friend and I've been less than attentive over the past few weeks, but I don't want you to get worried about me. Everything is going to be fine."

"Okay, if you really feel that way, then why did you ask me to stay here with you?"

"Kimmy, I just told you, you're my best friend and since I haven't been around as much as I should be, I thought this would be a good way for us to spend some time together."

"Yeah, whatever, I think you asked me to stay here because you saw the truck outside and were afraid, so you'd rather have someone else here with you than stay alone and take your chances with someone breaking in. I mean, what would you have done if I wasn't here and you came downstairs and found the front door wide open like it was?"

Riley sighed, "okay, maybe you're right. I didn't want to be here all alone, but that's only because it's a little spooky having someone park outside my house. I don't think whoever it is will try to break in; I just think they're watching the house. Why, I don't know, but I don't think that anyone is going to try and hurt either one of us."

Kim seemed to relax at that last comment. She agreed to stay, but only on the condition that Riley calls the police if the truck was still there first thing in the morning. Riley agreed.

Chapter 10

The girls decided to head out of the house for a while, figuring that the fresh air would do them good. Although neither one would say it, they both were curious to see what would happen with the truck when they pulled out of the driveway. Would it follow them? If so, would it be close enough to see who the driver was? Before they left, Riley rummaged through her backpack to find the number she had written down weeks before when she had gotten the crank call on her answering machine. She wanted to try to find out where the payphone was that the call came from, maybe then she could figure out who made the call in the first place. While Kim was changing, Riley dialed the operator and asked if she could find out more about the number. The operator told her that she was not able to give out that information, apologized and hung up. Riley was wandering through the house with the cordless phone in hand, trying to plan her next step, when she found herself standing in front of the double doors that guarded her father's office. Instinctively she reached out and turned the brass handles, the doors flew open with ease. As she stepped inside, memories came back to her, her father sitting behind his big desk, smoking his pipe, papers everywhere, one phone in his hand as he conferenced with someone else on speaker phone. No matter how busy he was, he always took a break when she came into the room. He would let her sit on his desk, even walk on it until she got to be too big, and sometimes he let her color on his expensive stationery. Those times with her dad were so precious to her, she did not realize how special those times were until this moment, the first time she had ever walked into the office and her father was not there. With the flash of memories came another important piece of information, her father's address book. Where was it? She pulled open the drawers on the antique desk until she found it. Tucked away in the back of the top drawer was what she was looking for. Her father's special address book, as he had called it. In it were numbers of people whose numbers did not exist, corporate executives, politicians, celebrities and even a former president or two were in there; but most importantly, the number to call to find out about numbers that didn't exist or needed to be traced, was in that book. Now, if she could only remember where it was listed. Riley flipped through the pages, running her index finger over each page, reciting the names and numbers, she was almost halfway through the book when she found the number she was looking for, labeled "lost and found" how clever her father was. She picked up the office extension and dialed the number, after the second ring a man's voice came on the line, "hello?"

Riley hesitated for a moment, then said, "hello? Who is this?"

The man replied, "you called me, who is this?"

She had nothing to lose, the number came from her father's book so what harm could possibly be done. She opened her mouth and spoke one long sentence that left her breathless, "I'm trying to locate a payphone, I have the number, can you help me?"

It was then the man's turn to hesitate. "Riley Matthews, is that you?"

She was stunned, so much so that she almost hung up the phone. "Who are you?"

"Riley, it's okay, I was a friend of your father's. The number comes up when you dial in. How did you find this number anyway?"

"My father told me about it a long time ago, and I really never thought about it again, but I'm having a bit of a situation going on and I really need to know where this payphone is. The operator couldn't help me, so I decided to take a chance and try to find this number. Can you help me?"

"What's the number?"

She recited the number, relaxing a little when he put her on hold to do some checking. She had no idea where she had called, but if the man on the phone could figure out who she was, she knew she had called someone important.

He came back almost instantly, "the number belongs to a phone booth registered to the Squeaky Hinge Bar and Grill, does that help at all?"

A little confused, Riley told him that the information helped and thanked him for his time. Before she could hang up, he told her that if she needed anything else, anything at all, she should call and ask for Gary. She thanked him again and hung up just as Kim walked into the room.

"Wow, you're dad sure had some office." Kim tossed herself down on one of the leather couches decorating the room. "Who were you talking to?"

Something told her that she would be better off not telling Kim about the number she had called, "the operator, I wanted to find out where the phone was that the woman called my house from."

"Oh, they'll never give you that information."

"Well, I guess the operator I talked to never heard that part of the rules. She gave me the address and everything."

"Lucky you. So where's the phone?"

"That's the weird part; it's at the Squeaky Hinge. Does that make any sense to you? Why would someone call me from the Squeaky Hinge and how did anyone there get my phone number in the first place?"

"I don't know what to tell you, maybe whoever it was called you by accident. Maybe they were trying to reach someone else."

"I thought of that. Now that I know the call came from the Squeaky Hinge I think that I was the person they were trying to call. It's too coincidental to be a wrong number."

"I guess you're right, but quite frankly if she didn't call back again I wouldn't be that concerned with it."

"Kim, you don't get it, do you? Ever since I came back here there has been a truck outside of the house. I got a strange threatening phone call from a phone at the Squeaky Hinge and none of this happened until you introduced me to Danny and his friends."

"What you really mean is none of this happened until you met Taylor."

"Okay, maybe that's what I mean. Don't you think that it all ties together?"

"No, I don't. I think you are overreacting to a situation that has gotten the best of your emotions. You liked Taylor, he caused you and Tony to break up, someone dials your number and leaves a crank call and now you think someone is out to get you? Get real, your imagination has gotten the best of you. You're freaked out at the truck in front of the house, but did you ever stop to think that whoever it is maybe watching the house and not watching you?"

Riley figured she'd tread lightly and give Kim some leeway as stressful situations did not bring out the best in Kim's logic. "Kim, you're making no sense, why would someone watch the house?"

"Riley, this house has been empty for a long time, suddenly there's movement and cars in the garage, no one but Sam and I know you're here. Maybe the neighbors are getting a little protective, thinking that someone is looting the house, or better yet, that someone knew the house was empty and decided to move in and make them a new home. Did you ever think of that? You know the neighborhood watch thing?"

Riley smiled, "Kim, you are so strange sometimes it scares me. Maybe you're right, maybe whoever it is thinks that something is wrong and that's why they are sitting outside. But then again, why haven't they called the police?"

It was now Kim's turn to hesitate, "not sure, maybe whoever it is just happens to be really slow."

"Very funny, I..." Riley's sentence was cut short by a banging on the front door. She looked at Kim.

"We'll never know until we open it," she said as she walked towards the front hall, Riley close behind.

"My parents are probably laughing out loud in heaven right about now. Little Riley, who would watch every horror movie she could get her hands on, was now afraid of a knock at the door, how pathetic."

"Oh, you're so right." Kim laughed.

Kim peaked out through the mirrored glass on the side of the doors as Riley looked though the peephole in the massive door. When she saw the two police officers, she could not help but call out, "who is it?"

"Riley!" Kim yelled in a hushed voice, "they're cops, open the door."

"Police, Ms. Matthews. We'd like to speak with you for a moment."

Riley cracked open the door, leaving the chain firmly in place. "What is it?"

The officers, one male and one female, were obviously not going to push the issue of the chain still being in place, in this neighborhood police were very respectful of the residents. "We received a call that there was a black truck sitting across the street for an extended period of time, we're just following up on it. Do you know anything about this?"

"Actually, I do. I'm not sure who is belongs to, but there was a black sport utility truck sitting in front of the house, it was there for hours and must have just pulled away because last time I checked it was still there."

"How long ago was that?"

"About fifteen minutes ago."

"You said it's been there for hours, why didn't you call us sooner?"

Riley did not feel like repeating the whole story to the police, especially since the more she talked about it, the dumber things were beginning to sound. "Look, whoever was in the truck was just sitting there. I figured they were enjoying the view or something. I didn't see the point in having someone come out here for no reason. The truck was not bothering me and it's gone now, so I don't think there is anything more to be said."

The officers apologized for bothering her and said goodbye. She closed the door and rebolted the lock.

"Enjoying the view? You have got to be kidding, Riley! That truck had you scared half to death."

"I know Kim, but the more we talk about it, the more I think that the whole thing is just one big coincidence and there's nothing for me to be concerned with, so let's forget about it and go get something to eat."

"Good idea, I'm starving."

They grabbed their bags and headed out towards the garage door. Riley clicked the remote to open the garage, her car still sitting on the driveway where she had left it hours earlier. They climbed in and opened the convertible top as they drove out the front gate. Kim turned on the radio and Riley joined in singing to the first song they both recognized, not paying any attention to the black truck as it appeared again three cars behind them as they turned onto the main road. The weather had turned from hot and humid to cool and breezy almost in an instant. "Hey Riley, I'm getting a little cold, would you mind if I put the top up?"

"Kim, you are such wimp, we'll be at the restaurant in five minutes just grab the sweatshirt off the back seat for now."

Kim undid her seatbelt and turned around in the seat to reach behind her, as she turned something caught her eye, the black truck. It was a few cars behind them one lane over, close enough for Kim to see the woman driving. Kim turned quickly and sat back down in the seat. "Riley, pull into that parking lot, quick!" She pointed to the right turn they were about to pass.

"Why?"

"Just do it!"

Riley turned the car into the lot and kept driving all the way around the building and into the underground garage. She pulled into a spot and put the car in park, turning the engine off. Kim was watching behind them, looking to see if any other cars were coming down the ramp. When she felt satisfied that no one had followed them into the garage, she relaxed.

"Kim, will you please tell me what that was all about?"

"I don't mean to scare you, but at this point I'm a little frightened so you might as well be scared too."

"What are you talking about?"

"When I reached back to get the sweatshirt, I noticed the black truck following us, and..."

Riley jumped in, "what, the truck was following us and you tell me to turn into a garage? How are we supposed to get out of here?"

"Relax, I saw the driver. It was a woman, and I know I've seen her before."

"You have?"

"Yes, but I don't know when or where. She looks really familiar, but I can't place her."

Riley started the car.

"Riley, what are you doing?"

"We've got to get out of here. This is ridiculous, I don't know what's going on, but I'm going to the police." She put the car in reverse and pulled out of the parking spot.

She drove to the top of the exit ramp, not knowing what to expect when she got there. Was the truck going to be sitting there, waiting for her? Who was this woman and what did she want with Riley? As the car rounded the turn leading to the street level of the parking lot, Riley breathed a sigh of relief as she saw no one in sight. Streetlights illuminated the lot, nothing was moving and there was no black truck waiting. She exited the lot on the north end, turning onto the main street and heading directly to the police station two blocks away.

They walked into the police station and found the two officers that had visited her house not even an hour before sitting at the main desk.

The male officer recognized her immediately, "Ms. Matthews, what brings you here?"

"I'd like to file a report," without thinking, those were the first words to come out of her mouth.

"Report about what?" He had stepped close enough to the counter she could read his name badge, Officer Sean Patrick.

"Officer Patrick, the truck you came to my house about... well, there may be more to the story then I let on. I wasn't sure at the time, but now I think I am."

"Sure about what?"

"I think whoever is in that truck is following me, stalking me if you will."

"Ms. Matthews, stalking is a big issue; you can't go around making accusations about someone stalking you without having evidence. Do you have any proof?"

"No, I mean, yes. I mean, I don't know. What do you consider proof?"

"Well, for starters, do you know who's driving the truck?"

"No."

"Why do you think someone is stalking you? Do you know who it is?"

"I don't know why and no, I don't know who it is."

Officer Patrick cracked a grin as he glanced at his partner who was now sitting at her desk listening intently to the conversation, as if it was the comic relief of her day. "Ms. Matthews, if you don't know who it is and have no idea why someone is following you, then there is nothing we can do."

Riley glared at the female officer, long and hard enough to cause her to turn back to the paperwork she had been working on when they arrived.

She then turned her attention back to Officer Patrick. "Officer, are you telling me that as a civil servant, you are not willing to document the complaints of one of your salary-paying taxpayers? Is that what you are saying? Because if that's what you're saying, get me your supervisor right now." Riley's statement was enough to get the officer to think twice about turning her away.

"He probably figured that you were some spoiled rich kid who had nothing better to do with your time then bother the cops. That's why he took your statement." Kim was right. The officer had finally appeased Riley by taking her long-winded statement and turning it into a few pages of her most vehement points. He wasn't interested in what she speculated about, as far as he was concerned, her fears were unwarranted and, therefore, he was not about to take her seriously. Riley signed the statement, better something small than nothing at all, was the thought that skipped though her mind as she and Kim walked out to the car.

Chapter 11

"Okay, so are you still up for dinner?"

"Kim, you are the only person I know who can eat anything at anytime."

"Is that a yes?"

Riley laughed. She was feeling a little better. They left the police station and even though Officer Patrick hadn't seemed to take her seriously, she now had a police report on file, whatever good it might do in the future, she didn't know, but at least it was there. "That was a yes, where do you want to go?"

"How about the Happy Carousel? We haven't eaten there since we were kids."

That made Riley laugh even harder. "There's a good reason we haven't eaten there since we were kids, the tables are miniature and there's a man walking around in a giant horse costume."

"So what if it's a kiddie joint, it'll be fun and we can certainly use some fun in our lives right now."

Riley agreed, she made a quick U-turn and drove towards the Happy Carousel. The place had been repainted since they had last been there, but it was still the same funky purple and pink with horses hanging from the rooftop. "Yuck, this paint job gets uglier every time I see it."

"No, it's always been ugly, just our tastes have improved with age."

"Sure Kimmy, whatever you say."

The inside smelled the same, fresh pizza, burgers, hot dogs, anything a starving kid could want or desire could be found at the Happy Carousel. Kim ordered a kiddie pizza with pepperoni while Riley opted for a cheeseburger with extra pickle. Neither of them could help smiling when the girl gave them their kiddie toys and remarked that they shouldn't give them to children under three.

"I can't believe that cashier thinks we're old enough to have kids of our own," Riley said.

"Could be worse, Riley, she could have ma'am'd us too."

They took their food and found a table on the upstairs balcony overlooking the strip of little stores that lined the street. Finally a little more relaxed, hunger overtook them and they ate ravenously, Riley popped the last bite of her cheeseburger into her mouth and was sipping her soda as she glanced out over the sea of people walking the street. Kim seemed to be doing the same thing, people watching, when she and Riley found themselves noticing the same person.

"Hey, Riley, isn't that Taylor?"

Riley had noticed the man sitting outside at one of the shops along the street, he had a newspaper in his hand, but seemed more intent on looking over it than reading it.

"That's who it looks like, but I'm not sure, can't really see clearly from here."

"What a coincidence, I mean, what would he be doing in this part of town?"

"He lives not too far from here, maybe he comes here a lot, it's not like we would know, we haven't been here in years."

Kim stared at Riley as she asked her next question, "how do you know where he lives?"

"I told you he and I met several times, we talked a lot, he told me that they lived around here somewhere, I'm not exactly sure where though."

"Riley, I don't know what's going on, but I'm getting the feeling you stumbled onto something more involved than just a fling with a married man."

Riley thought about what Kim had said, there was more to this story, she was right, but Riley was not sure she wanted to know what was going on. Maybe it was best if she let things be and went on with her life, maybe then Taylor and the black truck would go away and she could have some semblance of a normal life again. Fed up with the situation, she decided that her parents had built a home secure enough to keep people out and she was going to use that security to her best advantage. Standing up, she took her tray and headed towards the trashcan. "Let's go."

Kim followed without asking questions. She seemed to know that when Riley was in this kind of mood there was no stopping her and no point in trying to discuss the situation with her. It was obvious that Riley was annoyed at the unexpected turns her life was taking, she was a control freak, and with strange things happening that she did not have control of, fear would turn to annoyance quickly. They drove back to the house in silence, both equally aware of the black truck following close behind. Riley drove through the gate and made sure it closed completely before pulling into the garage. She locked the garage door and entered the house, triggering the alarm. The screeching sound was so loud that Kim pushed her hands over her ears. "Riley, turn that thing off!"

It was as if a superior being overtook Riley, she walked into the hallway in a trance-like state letting the alarm continue until the buzzer by the front door began to ring in synch with the telephone. Riley punched in the alarm code on the keypad and then held her palm up to the pad to be scanned before the alarm stopped screeching. She answered the buzzer first, "Who is it?"

"Beach patrol, Ms. Matthews, responding to the alarm."

She looked at the screen, recognizing the vehicle as one of the patrols from the area, she buzzed open the gate for him. At the same time, answering the telephone. "Hello?"

"This is Officer Sean Patrick from the Manalapan police department. Is everything okay up there?"

Riley groaned. Officer Patrick, of all the officers in the department, the only one who couldn't take her seriously would have to be the one to call on the alarm, how lucky could she get. "Yes, Officer, everything is fine, the alarm went off and I had not gotten to the keypad to turn it off quickly enough, sorry for bothering you.

"No bother, just wanted to make sure you were okay. If you need anything, give a holler this way. Have a nice evening." Dial tone. He hung up before she could respond to him. For some reason, she felt better knowing he was there. He seemed almost sincere in his words, wanting to make sure she was okay. Suddenly, she felt guilty about bad mouthing him. Oh, well, she made a mental note to be nicer to him next time she saw him. Just then someone knocked on the front door, "police, open up!"

"Coming." She peeked through the window on the side of the door and saw two officers in beach patrol uniforms. She unlocked the deadbolt and chain, swinging the door open.

"Hi," she said.

"Ms. Matthews?"

"Yes."

"We're responding to the alarm. Are you alright?"

"Just fine, thank you. I accidentally set off the alarm. I'm sorry you had to come out here for nothing."

"Do you mind if we come in and take a look around?"

Riley hesitated at first, but then decided since she started this charade she might as well go all the way with it. "Sure, come in, look around all you want."

The officers entered, scanning the hallway they saw Kim sitting on the steps where she had been since this whole thing started. At first the confused look on Kim's face said she was unsure of what Riley was doing, but Riley caught Kim's eye and winked. It was that action that made it obvious to Kim that Riley was annoyed with being followed and she was going to use any method she could to show the driver of the truck that there was excellent security around the house and that she was not afraid to make the best usage of it. The driver had made her move by showing up wherever they had gone, this was Riley's move, she was now saying, "if you want to play, be careful because I'm in the mood for a challenge."

The officers searched the house from top to bottom, satisfied they had done their job thoroughly; they called into the alarm company and assured them that everything was secure. Then they left; not before reminding Riley to lock the deadbolt and chain before activating the alarm. Riley did as they said, locking the door after they left. She even watched to make sure they left through the front gate and no one entered behind them. Then she activated the alarm and perimeter lights, making sure no one could get into the house unannounced. Then she turned to Kim. "I don't know about you, but I'm ready for bed."

Kim stood up slowly, "Riley, what are you doing? This house is a fortress; no one could get in without you letting them in. Why the big security measures?"

"Kim, I don't know who's out there, but quite frankly, I'm going to watch out for my own butt! If you don't like the way I'm living in my own house, then leave." Kim saw the back of Riley's head as she whizzed passed her and up the stairs, the next she heard was Riley closing her bedroom door.

Kim was scared, not of the weird events, but of the way Riley had started to act. She did not know this woman anymore; this was not her best friend, the one she had grown up with, the person she had told her secrets to. As much as she wanted to help, she felt Riley needed to handle this on her own at least that is the way Riley was making her feel. She went upstairs and packed her things. Even though it was close to midnight, she felt it best if she left quietly now instead of waiting until the morning. She wrote out a note explaining why she couldn't stay, and telling Riley that she would always be there for her, but right now Riley was too focused to need or want anyone else in her life. Kim hoped she phrased her note in a way that Riley would understand and not be hurt. There was nothing else she could do now, so she took her bags and left through the back door, resetting the alarm as she left.

Riley heard Kim's car start as she pulled out of the driveway. Maybe it was best if Kim left. Riley was too concerned with herself right now and even though this morning asking Kim to stay here seemed to be a good idea, as the day's events progressed, the idea seemed like less of a good one.

She climbed out of bed and peaked out of the window, watching the gate close behind Kim as she turned onto the main road.

Riley scanned the area for the truck but to no avail, the driver would have to sleep sometime and maybe the alarm going off and the police arriving was enough to scare her away, for tonight at least; Riley was pretty sure that tomorrow morning would find the truck right back in front of the house.   She would deal with that in the morning, for now, she was exhausted, time to sleep.   She shut off the bedroom lights, leaving the bathroom light on to be able to see in the middle of the night, she told herself. Although the real reason was that she was still afraid.

She dozed off quickly into a fitful sleep, tossing and turning as she tried to rest her tired body.

The sun shining through the curtains woke her at 8:30. She had slept soundly and was feeling very refreshed when she woke up. Grabbing her robe, she washed up in the bathroom before heading down to the kitchen for some breakfast.

Curiosity got the better of her as she walked past the front hallway, pulling back the curtains she noticed that there was no one parked in front of the house.

"Slacking off," she joked to herself as she pulled down a bowl for her cereal. She was in mid bite when an idea struck her. If there was no one to see her leave, she could turn the tables on whoever is following her and gather more information for the police.

She left her dishes sitting on the table and ran upstairs. Riley could not remember the last time she showered and dressed so quickly. She was out of the house within 30 minutes, record time for her.

She had seen Kim's note on the table, and made herself a mental reminder to call her later. She did not want Kim to think that she was mad at her for leaving; in fact she understood exactly why Kim had left. Riley didn't want to be around someone who was as focused as she was right now, she knew she was not a fun person to be around and therefore she didn't expect Kim to stay around either. They would make up later; Riley knew that when this whole thing blew over, they could go back to being the best friends they were before whatever this started. Riley went to the garage, pulling her car out onto the driveway, she parked in plain view of the spot where the truck had been sitting. Then she grabbed a bottle of soda, a pad, pen and her cell phone before walking out behind the house. She circled around and found herself a little spot behind the hedges where she had a view of the front of the house. She checked her watch, 10 o'clock, she wondered how long it would take before something happened. She found herself exhilarated by the idea of surveillance, not knowing what would occur. She chuckled softly as the thought of "Riley Matthews, Private Investigator" drifted through her mind. Hesitating for a moment, she quickly regained her focus and returned to the task at hand. Her plan was to obtain as much information as she could, without letting on that she was there. A license plate number should be sufficient and if she could get a look at the driver that would even be better. She figured that she could take the information to the police and then Officer Patrick would have to follow-up on it. He wanted proof; well she would get him proof!

It was almost an hour later when something finally happened, although it was not what Riley had fully expected. Her initial expectation had been that the truck would show up so she could get the information she needed, sneak back into the house, then leave through the garage and go to the police. In fact, the reason she had left her car outside was specifically so that the driver would think she was home, if there was no car there, the driver might not stay for very long. What Riley expected and what she saw where two totally different things. She saw the truck drive up the main road past her hiding spot in the bushes, the driver, still a woman, was following behind a few other cars being led by a flatbed pickup truck. Riley did not think much about it until the four or five cars stopped, she was not sure why they were stopping since there was nothing coming the opposite way and there were no turn offs for at least 3 miles past her house. She noticed the pickup truck was pulling into an opening between the trees on the far side of her property. Once the pickup was nestled into it's hiding spot between the trees the other cars continued down the road, just in time for Riley to see the black truck that had been watching her house pull into the same spot it had been sitting in previously. The oddness of the situation struck her as she realized the woman driving the black sport utility truck was not watching her, she was watching the pickup truck, and once Riley took a good look at the pickup truck she realized the driver was none other than Taylor! Now she was confused. Taylor had somehow found her house and was stalking her, as scary as that was, it made sense, the other truck did not make any sense at all. Why would someone be watching Taylor? And more importantly, who was it? Riley crawled along the hedges until she was close enough to read the license plate on the black truck. She wrote it down on the pad she brought with her. She tried to make out the driver, but could only see that it was a woman with black hair pulled back in a braid down to the base of her neck. Riley did not want to risk getting any closer for fear of being seen, so she took her information and crawled back along the hedges to the back of the house. As she came around the back of the house she realized she had no way of getting into the house without being seen, the garage was the only door she had left open and in order to get in through the garage she would have to walk out onto the driveway in plain view of both Taylor and the mysterious driver. She was about to break a window when she spotted a towel lying over a beach chair in the corner of the yard. Without thinking, she grabbed the towel and shook it out. She stripped down to her undies and bra and wrapped the towel around her. Then she turned the hose on and shivered as the cold water ran over her hair. When she was done, she was satisfied that anyone seeing her would think she came out of the water, the fact that the pool was not filled would be irrelevant since there was an entire ocean behind her house, no one would be the wiser. She tucked her clothing under her arm and walked out onto the driveway, it took all of her restraint not to look out towards the road or through the trees to see if anyone was watching her. She knew they were there, she could feel Taylor's eyes on her, watching her as she entered the garage. She closed the door behind her and went into the house, breathing a sigh of relief as she reset the alarm. Riley changed back into her clothes and dried her hair. She picked up the phone to call Officer Patrick, but decided it would be better if she went there in person to talk with him. She grabbed the notebook she had written the license plate down on and was about to leave the house when she thought of the picture of Taylor she had in a box upstairs from the band flyer. It might be helpful she thought, although she was sure that he was no danger to her, he was just lonely. From what he had told her, his wife took their daughter and went back to her parents in Detroit, thinking that it would be better for the little girl to be in a loving environment until the divorce details were worked out. He was weird, but harmless Riley thought, but whoever the other person was, she had no idea if there was danger involved or not. She decided not to take any chances and if that meant getting Taylor involved in the investigation then so be it, he would understand. She ran upstairs and sifted through boxes looking for the band flyer she had shoved into her bag at the Squeaky Hinge not too long ago. She went through all of the boxes, finally in the last one she found it, she smoothed it out, refolded it neatly and put it in her pocket.

As she pulled away from the gate and onto the main road, she noticed both Taylor and the black truck were gone.

Chapter 12

It only took her a few minutes to get to the police station, traffic was light for the weekend this time of year. Just as she was pulling into the station house her cell phone rang. She grabbed it thinking it might be Tony, she hadn't called him since she moved out and as annoyed as he was, he would still be concerned that he had not heard from her. She pushed the talk button, "hello?"

"Riley, don't hang up, it's me, Taylor."

She cringed. "What do you want?"

"I just want to talk to you. I know last time we spoke you said you didn't want to talk to me anymore, but I really need to talk with you, can you meet me right now?"

"Right now? Taylor look, I really don't have anything left to say to you, so I'm not sure why you would want me to meet you."

"I know you're angry, but I really think if we talk, we can work things out. At least we could be friends if nothing more. Please meet me."

Against her best instincts, Riley relented. "I'll meet you, but not now. I'm about to get my hair cut and if I'm late it will take weeks to get another appointment." She lied, figuring it was best if he not know where she was.

"Okay, later will be okay, if getting your haircut is really that important to you." It was almost as if he knew exactly where she was and was trying to prevent her from going to the police.

She decided to appease him; after all he might be able to give her some answers as to what was going on. "Taylor, if it's that important, then I'll postpone my appointment, but it'll be about an hour before I can meet you, figuring that she needed at least that much time to talk with the police.

"Okay, I'll meet you in an hour at the same place we met last time."

"I'll be there, and don't get worried if I'm a few minutes late, punctuality is not my strong point these days, okay?"

"Agreed, I'll see you later."

She ended the call and got out of the car. She was just about to walk into the police station when something caught her eye; Taylor's truck was parked in a lot across from the police station! She pulled open the door and went inside, her heart racing, she ran up the stairs to the sergeant's desk and asked for Officer Patrick. The desk sergeant said he was busy, and offered another officer to help her, but she insisted he call him again, this time telling the officer that Riley Matthews was here.

He appeared within moments, coming through the side door in plain clothes. He looked more appealing out of uniform, and for a brief moment, Riley found him attractive, then she remembered why she was there.

"Ms. Matthews, how can I help you?"

"Officer Patrick, I need to talk with you privately, it's very important."

He must have sensed the fear in her voice, because he did not hesitate, he turned to the desk sergeant and told him he would be back shortly. Then he extended his arm out towards the doorway he had entered through, "after you."

Riley walked through the doorway into a hallway with offices on each side. He directed her to a small lunchroom asking the two officers sitting at the table to excuse them, they left closing the door behind them, she was now alone with Officer Patrick.

He pulled out her chair and they sat. "So, how can I help you, Ms. Matthews?"

"Well, first of all, please call me Riley."

"Okay, Riley, how can I help you?"

"Well, when I was here last time you said you needed proof that someone was following me before you could do anything. So, I got you proof."

"Proof in one day, I'm impressed. Pray tell, what is your proof?"

Tears came to her eyes, she did not know why, but he realized she was upset and his humor was not helping the situation. The day before she had been almost arrogant with him, today was different, she was afraid and her fear was now obvious.

"Riley, I'm sorry, I did not mean to make light of the situation. What is it that you have?"

She rummaged through her pocket and found the picture of Taylor, then she laid the piece of notebook paper with the license plate number on it next to the picture on the table, "here."

"What is all this? A picture and a piece of paper?"

"The paper has the license plate number of the black truck that has been sitting outside of my house for days and the picture is of the man I dated briefly who was also sitting in front of my house this morning."

He looked at her intently, she was obviously serious about someone following her, but he did not realize that there were two people involved in this surveillance. He grabbed a piece of paper off of the shelf and began to take note.

"Okay, let's start at the beginning," he said.

She seemed relieved that someone was taking her seriously, and the story then to flow from her.

"I was engaged to one guy and then met this other man through a friend of mine, Kim, the one that was here with me yesterday.

Anyway, he and I hit it off and we began seeing each other. This other guy, Taylor, was, is, married and his wife and he have since split; she's in Detroit somewhere with their daughter. Things got strange with him. He started acting a little possessive, so I broke it off, told him I never wanted to see him again. Then I broke things off with my fiancée' because, well, let's just say it obviously wasn't working out.

I moved out yesterday and noticed that this black sport utility truck has been parked in front of my house, I don't know if it was following me before I moved or not, but it's been there positively since yesterday.

This morning I decided to sneak around and get the license plate so you, the police, could find out more about what is going on. While I was out there, I saw the truck pull up and park in its usual spot, but this time there was more to it.

The woman driving the sport utility seemed to be following a pickup truck that was parking in the trees along the side of the property, and the driver of that truck was Taylor. Then the final thing happened when I pulled into the station parking lot, my cell phone rang and it was Taylor. He wanted me to meet him immediately, but I told him I had plans and couldn't, so he persisted and I told him I'd meet him in an hour or so. Then as I came in the front door, I saw his truck parked across the street."

Officer Patrick seemed stunned at what she had just told him. There was obviously something going on, someone was keeping tabs on her. It seemed as if this Taylor guy was watching her, something that happened everyday by men who were rejected, they hung around for a while, then usually disappeared, the rare cases involved the police and the very rare cases the coroner, but never had he heard of a woman watching a man who was watching his ex-girlfriend, this was definitely out of the ordinary.

"Are you saying that the guy is across the street right now?"

"I'm not sure, all I know is that his truck was at my house, then it was gone when I left to come here and when I got here he called me. His truck was across the street, I didn't see him." She felt better knowing that he was taking her seriously. She glanced at her watch, "I'm supposed to meet him in a half hour, I'm willing to bet if I don't show, he'll be outside when I leave here."

He paused as if he was thinking about what she had just said, Riley was frustrated and about to say something when he finally spoke up.

"You wait here." He took the paper with the tag number and walked out the door, closing it behind him. She looked around the kitchen area; it was empty except for a few vending machines and a microwave. Fumbling in her pockets she found three quarters and bought herself a Coke. She had just opened the can when Office Patrick came back into the room.

"Riley, I talked to my supervisor and he wants you to meet this guy."

Now it was her turn to be stunned, "are you serious?"

"He thinks it would be a good idea. We could follow him and find out more about what's going on. There would be an officer at your house at all times for the next 24 hours, so you'd be safe, and you said yourself that you didn't think he posed any danger to you."

"I know what I said, but do you really think all that is necessary? Couldn't you just arrest him and the woman following him and talk to them?"

"Riley, we don't know who the woman is."

"I gave you the license plate number, can't you find out that way?" She was on the verge of tears, this was not going as planned, they wanted to use her as bait and she did not know why.

"The truck is rented, and the name is fake. We have no idea who the woman is, I'm sorry."

"So this is the only way?"

"Unfortunately, yes."

She composed herself and agreed to go meet Taylor, "on one condition," she said.

"What?"

"You have to be the officer following me." She did not know why she said what she did, but she seemed more comfortable knowing he would be watching after her, only a few steps away in case anything happened.

He smiled, "agreed." He looked at his watch; it was almost time for her to meet Taylor. "Let's get you set up."

"Set up?"

"We're going to put a wire on you so we can hear everything you two say."

"A wire? Do you really think that's a good idea?"

"It'll work just fine, nothing to worry about. Now, where are you supposed to meet him?"

Riley gave him the location and was left alone with the female officer that had come into the room. Officer Patrick said his good-byes and told her not to worry, he was going to leave the station now and head over to the meeting place. He did not want Taylor to see them leaving together. Riley managed a smile and a goodbye as he left.

The female officer, Officer Jackson, then explained to Riley how the wire worked and taped it to her body under her bra. She made sure to emphasize that Riley should not let him touch her, the wire would not be detectable from sight, but if he touched it, he would be able to feel it.

Riley couldn't help being a little offended by the officer's remarks and promptly replied, "Officer Jackson, I don't know about you, but I don't usually let men fondle my breasts in public, therefore I don't think we have to be concerned with him touching the wire, do you?"

The officer stepped back, apologizing to Riley she opened the door as if to signal she knew she had overstepped her bounds and it was time for her to leave. Riley walked to the front door and left, glancing across the street she noticed the truck was gone, then she noticed it was almost time to meet Taylor, if she hurried she could still be on time.

Walking quickly, she jumped into the car, started the engine and headed off towards the beach. Traffic was still light so she had enough time to park and brush her hair before she saw him pull in. He parked the truck and walked over to her car as she got out. He leaned over and gave her a kiss on the cheek to say hello.

"I'm glad you agreed to meet me."

"Taylor, I'm only here because you said it was important." She hoped by keeping things abrupt, he would not try to touch her, she had no desire to be touched by him and she was intending to make that perfectly clear.

"Riley, it is important, I miss you. I want us to give it one more try. To have a relationship."

"Taylor, I can't have a relationship with you. I'm afraid of you, your mood swings, your controlling attitude, I never know what to expect next and I won't live like that."

"Riley, you hardly know me, please give me another chance and I will show you how good I can be to you, how good we can be together."

She didn't know where the courage she had was coming from, but she figured it was the knowledge that Officer Patrick was somewhere close, making her feel safe. She looked him straight in the eyes, "Taylor, you're right, I don't know you that well, but I do know that since we have met, things have been strange and I don't like that. My life may not have been perfect, but at least I know that before we met, I had some semblance of control in my life, you have managed to make things very uncomfortable for me and I don't like that." She was about to tell him to get lost, but then realized that it might be in her best interests not to totally anger him. "Taylor, look, if it's that important to you, we can be friends, but I can't date you, at least not now.

When things settle down with Jeni, we can talk, but until the divorce is final, we can't date. Is that fair?"

A grimace seemed to come over his face, as if he was satisfied with the offer, for now at least. "That's fair, for now, but once the divorce is final I want to talk more about us getting serious."

Riley's stomach turned, but she managed to keep her cool. "That's fine, we'll talk more then. Right now, I have to go, I have a commitment and I'm going to be late if I don't get a move on."

He leaned over again and kissed her on the cheek. "I'll call you soon."

She watched as he walked over to his truck, got in and drove off. She jumped at the tap on her window, and was relieved to see Officer Patrick standing there. She rolled down the window.

"That was great," he said.

"What happens now?"

"The other officers will follow him and we'll see what turns up. As for you, go about your day and don't be surprised to see me following you around." He smiled.

'He has a nice smile,' she thought. She thanked him and drove off, hesitating long enough for him to get into his car and fall into his place a few cars behind her. She pulled out her "to do" list and was trying to prioritize when her cell phone rang again. She stared at it briefly, hesitating to answer it in case it was Taylor.

Finally, the ringing got the best of her and she answered, "hello?"

"Riley, it's Tony. How are you?"

She was relieved to hear his voice, "I'm okay, just been having one of those days, if you know what I mean."

"It's been like that for me since you left. I'm sorry I wasn't there, but the thought of you moving out was too much for me and I really didn't want to be there while you packed. Can you forgive me?"

"Tony, I know this is hard. It's hard for me too, but we'll get through it, I promise. As for you not being there when I left, it was probably easier for both of us that way."

"Thanks, I needed to hear that. So, where are you staying?"

"I went back to my parent's house. It's about time I went back and faced my past."

"Are you okay? I mean being in the house alone?"

"I'm not alone."

"You're not?" He seemed a little upset at the thought of her being with someone else, of course he wouldn't think that she might have security or a housekeeper, his mind was on Taylor and he figured that she had asked this guy to move in with her. He couldn't be further from the truth.

"No, I'm not. Sam is still there and right now there are some things going on that require security, so there's a police officer on duty round the clock."

His attitude changed quickly when he heard her say police on duty, "Riley, is everything okay? What is going on that requires you to have police there all the time? Has someone threatened you?" His concern was obvious.

"No, nothing like that." She decided to level with him, she owed him honesty and she had no reason to lie to him now. "There's been a sport utility truck following me and it turns out that the driver is following a pickup truck that happens to belong to someone I know. So right now the police are trying to figure out what's going on without letting these people in on the fact they are being tailed by the cops."

"A sport utility? By any chance is it black with a woman driver?"

Riley pulled off to the side of the road, this conversation had just taken an unexpected turn and she was not sure what to expect next. "What makes you think that?"

"Well, about a week or so ago a woman in a black sport utility came by and knocked on the door. She said she was looking for the woman of the house, and I told her to come back another day."

"Tony, did you give her my name?"

"I know I told her Riley, but I don't remember if I said Matthews or not. Riley, I'm sorry, did she find out who you were because of me?"

"I don't know, maybe. She probably took the name off the mailbox or something. Once she knew my first name, checking the mail for my last would not have been too difficult to do. At least that explains how she got some of the information. How she got to the house is still beyond me."

"Where did you meet the guy she's following?"

"At the Squeaky Hinge."

"Well, if she's following him, I'm sure she knows by now where he lives, maybe she followed you home one night instead of him and that's how she found you. Now, if she's at the house on the beach, that's probably because she followed you from here the other day."

Riley realized the importance of what Tony had just said. If this woman had followed her from the Squeaky Hinge then she had seen her with Taylor. Who knows how long she had been following her. And she was probably the one who made the crank phone call. But why? Maybe the woman was Jeni? That couldn't be, Jeni was in Detroit with her parents and their daughter. Taylor would know that she was here. No, whoever this woman was, she knew Taylor and now knew Riley was part of his life, so she was gathering information for something, but what? "Tony, listen, I have to go. I'll call you later and we can talk more, okay."

"Tonight's not good, I'm working. Actually, it might be best if we hold off on talking for a while, let things settle down. Of course, if you need my help with this situation, let me know, but other than that, how about I call you later in the week?"

"Fair enough, I'll talk with you then." She hung up the phone and took a deep breath; it seemed that at every turn there was more to the story than she had anticipated. It was like a ball of yarn that was unwinding faster and faster as it rolled down stairs. She thought of calling Officer Patrick, then she remembered the wire. Talking out loud, she said, "Officer Patrick, can you hear me?"

Yes Riley, loud and clear" was his reply through her earpiece.

"Did you hear that conversation?" She didn't know how clear the cell phone was or if it could be heard over the wire.

"Only your end of it."

"Well, I think we should meet so I can tell you the other part of it. It has to do with the woman in the sport utility."

"Pull your car around to the back of the parking lot, I'll meet you there."

She turned the engine on and pulled the car to the back of the lot as he instructed. There were enough cars there to allow hers to melt into the background. Officer Patrick pulled up next to her a moment later.

"Wow, you weren't kidding when you said you'd be following me around."

He smiled as he hopped into the front seat next to her.

"Okay, what's the scoop?" He asked.

"The call was from Tony, my ex. He said that there was a woman in a black sport utility truck that came to our house a few weeks back. She didn't say what she wanted other than to ask him to speak to the woman of the house. He gave her my name and told her to come back another time when I'd be home. She never came back. Tony didn't think anything of it at the time, but when I told him that there was a truck following me, he remembered the incident. What do you think it means? Why would she have been at my house?"

He thought for a moment, "I'm not really sure why she'd be there. Honestly, I thought it was the wife following her husband and trying to catch him having an affair or something, but obviously there's more to it. The woman is definitely not his wife."

"How do you know that for sure?"

"We ran a few reports and pulled info from the dmv. His wife is a blond and about six inches taller than the woman in the truck. This woman is only about five foot two Jeni is five foot eight. The other tidbit is that his wife is, well, let's just say she's well proportioned, this woman is more of the typical woman, very average build. We've been trying to track down Jeni, but from what you told us, he said she was with her parents in Detroit..."

"That's what Taylor said. She took Kelsey, their daughter, and went to her parents for a while, until the divorce was final."

"Riley, I don't doubt you; it's just that we are having a problem finding Jeni and Kelsey."

"How difficult can it be to find her parents, Detroit may be a big city, but it can't be that big!"

"No, that's not the problem. The problem is that Jeni's parents died in a fire three years ago."

Riley stared at him. "What? How can they be dead? Taylor said she went to stay with them. He would know if there were dead."

"I agree. We've come up with one of two scenarios. First, Taylor never knew Jeni's parents were dead because she never told him, and now she's using the lie of being with them to get away from him. Or the other scenario is that he lied to you about where Jeni is."

"Why would he lie to me? All he had to do was tell me she left him, I wouldn't have questioned him."

"No, but he had no way of knowing what you would ask. By telling you that she's with her parents, the story sounds plausible and you probably wouldn't have asked anything more about it. If he had only said she left, he was taking the chance that you would ask where she went, and if you asked one question, there might be more and that was a risk he wasn't going to take."

"What do you mean by risk he wasn't going to take? You make him sound like some sort of criminal."

"Riley, we ran a background check on your friend Taylor. He's not exactly Mr. Clean."

"What does that mean?"

"He's got a record. Back a few years, he was arrested for assault and battery in Michigan. The charges were dropped when he plea-bargained and agreed to leave town. The next place he landed was Florida and he ran into trouble here as well. I can't tell you the details, but this guy has a violent temper and it seems that wherever he goes, someone gets physically hurt."

"I don't believe that. He's a little off, but I can't believe he's violent." As she said the words her mind flashed back to the day on the beach when Taylor grabbed her arm. She remembered how scared she was that he was going to hurt her. Maybe Office Patrick was right, he was violent.

"Riley?"

"Yeah, I was just thinking, nothing important. You said that wherever he goes someone gets hurt, but no one got hurt this time, right?" She asked the question, but was not too sure she wanted to hear the answer.

"Riley, right now I can't answer that. Until we know who's driving the sport utility truck and can make sure Jeni and Kelsey are okay... there are no certain answers yet. We should know something soon and as soon as I know, I'll tell you whatever I can."

"I just hope everyone is alright and this thing ends quickly."

"I want that as well. For now, it might be best if I take you back to your place and we call it quits for today. It will be easier for someone to watch you when you're at home in one place instead of moving around in crowded areas."

"Sure. That makes sense. But my house is big enough that you don't have to hang out outside, you can watch out for me from inside. Wouldn't that be a better idea?" Riley knew she was being brazen, but for some reason she didn't think twice about making the suggestion.

"Riley, that's really nice of you, but the officer on duty is supposed to be outside of the house, it's a more ideal way to watch for things out of the ordinary."

She smiled at him, a flirtatious grin, "well, you've been on duty all day, so the night shift must belong to someone else, right?"

"Yes, that would be Officer Jackson."

"Okay then, let Officer Jackson stand watch outside and you and I can enjoy some home cooking inside. Deal?" She had no idea where this courage was coming from, especially since she had no idea if he was married or attached or anything of the sort. He answered her quickly.

"I'd love to."

She got her answer, he was obviously not attached. "Well, I'd better get going if I'm going to fix dinner. Why don't you meet me at the house at seven?"

"Seven sounds good, I'll be there." He closed the car door behind him and she watched him climb into his unmarked patrol car and drive off toward the station.

As she pulled out of the parking lot, she noticed the black truck was back and so was Taylor's pickup. However, the thing neither of the other drivers noticed was the unmarked police cruiser driven by Officer Jackson following all of them.

Chapter 13

Riley made it home in record time, she felt more secure knowing that there was a police officer following her at all times and that Officer Patrick would be at her home soon enough. She pulled through the gate, waiting for it to close completely before pulling in front of the garage. The two trucks, still unaware of each other, parked in their usual spots while Officer Jackson parked down the road in a wooded area so not to be seen by either of the truck's drivers.

Riley entered the house, triggering the motion sensors which caused the house to light up like the fourth of July. The phone began ringing almost at the same instant as the lights came on. She grabbed the extension in the laundry room. "Hello?"

"Riley, it's Kim. Everything okay?"

Riley was relieved to hear a friendly voice on the other end, "yes, I'm okay. It's been a wild day though."

"Listen, I'm sorry I left so quickly. The whole thing just spooked me and I went chicken on you. I'm really sorry. If you want, I'll come back and stay with you."

"Kim, that's really sweet, and I totally understand why you left. For now, I think I can handle things here by myself. I went to the police again today, this time with the license plate of the truck and they were able to help me, so everything's under control."

"What did they say? Do they know who it is following you?"

"That's the strange part," she paused. "Kim, hang on for a minute, I'm going to switch phones."

"Sure."

Riley put the call on hold and went into the kitchen to get the cordless. That way she could talk and fix dinner at the same time. "Kim, you there?"

"I'm here. So, tell me what the strange thing was."

"It seems as though the black truck isn't following me after all. The woman is following Taylor. It's Taylor who led her to me, he's the one following me!"

"What! That's crazy. Why would some woman be following Taylor? And why would Taylor be following you? Hey, maybe the woman is his wife and she's trying to catch him having a fling?"

"Nope, nice guess though. The police can't find Jeni or figure out who the woman is, she rented the truck and the name is a fake. Right now the cops are watching the house, and I don't think they are planning to do anything more until they find Jeni and Kelsey."

"So what are you doing? Just hanging out at home being watched by a dozen eyes?" Kim laughed at her own attempt at humor.

"Very funny. If you really want to know though, I have a dinner date for this evening."

"Oh, how creepy is that? The cops are going to get to watch you fooling around with some guy?"

"No, there won't be any fooling around, and the guy happens to be a cop himself."

"No way! You got a date with the cop from the station?"

"How did you know?"

"Riley, please, he's so your type! I just can't believe you moved so fast!"

Kim was right, she was moving a little fast, the moment had a hold of her and she felt drawn to this man. There was something about him that comforted her, something that told her they were supposed to meet. What would come of it, she couldn't predict, but something was telling her he was supposed to be in her life. "Maybe you're right, it happened a little fast, but it's just dinner and that's all. With this whole situation going on, I'm sure he understands that I'm vulnerable and he won't take advantage of the situation."

"I'm sure he'll understand, in fact, he'll most likely be really cautious and distant. Don't take it personally if he is, okay?"

"Understood. I'll just play it by ear and have a nice relaxed evening."

"Good idea. And Riley?"

"Yes?"

"After your nice relaxed evening, call me with the details!"

"Kim, I'd love to, but I can't."

"What? I'm you're best friend and you're not going to tell me what happens?"

"It's not that, the thing is the cops have my phones tapped and the car wired, so if I call you the whole world will know what happened. Trust me, once this blows over, if there is anything to tell, I'll tell you."

"Alright. I'd better let you go fix dinner. Call me tomorrow."

"Alright, bye."

As she hung up the phone, it rang again almost instantaneously making her jump. Her hand a little shaky, she reached for the receiver again. "Hello?"

This time the caller was not a friendly voice. "Riley, it's me. I need to talk to you."

The urgency in Taylor's voice was clear, but what unnerved her even more was the fact that he was calling on her home line. This number was unlisted and she had never given it to him. In fact, even Tony did not have this number, only Kim and a few select associates of her father. Everyone else had always been given the main number and that phone was always answered by voicemail. She gathered her thoughts quickly, not wanting to let on that something was wrong. "Taylor, what is it?"

"I can't talk long, it's really important that we meet somewhere private. Maybe I could come to your house?"

Her house? He must be crazy! She was not letting him into the house, that was for sure. He was becoming very forward in his attempts to see her. She had never told him where she lived, or that she lived in a house as opposed to an apartment. He was obviously not thinking clearly, and she was well aware that he was right outside of the house, only a hundred yards or so. Officer Jackson would also be out there, and she should be able to hear this conversation over her tapping devices.

"Taylor, I don't think it's a good idea that you call here. I have guests right now and I can't talk. Why don't you give me a number where I can reach you tomorrow?"

The line was quiet, it seemed like he was thinking over her offer.

"Taylor, did you want to give me a number or not?" This time her voice was firm, she wanted to make it clear that she was not talking to him right now and he had only one option left.

He rattled off a phone number that Riley was sure would end up being a cellular phone, but she took it anyway, any information she could get for the police would be helpful. She said a quick good-bye and hung up the phone. She almost didn't answer it when it rang again almost immediately, but then noticing the clock, she glanced at the gate monitor and saw Officer

Patrick sitting at the gate. She buzzed him in, telling him to use the back entrance, Taylor did not need to see who was coming and going in her home.

He pulled up quietly and parked the cruiser in back. She opened the back door to let him in, noticing he was carrying a bakery box, she smiled. "Sweets for the sweet," he said as he handed it to her.

"Can I peek?"

"Sure."

She opened a corner of the box and the smell of fresh baked apple pie filled the room.

"Apple pie, my favorite. How did you know?" She laughed at her own question. "Oh, let me guess, you investigated me too?"

"Not quite. I've always loved apple pie and I figured that no matter what you made for dinner, the pie would compliment it nicely."

"Works for me. I guess apple pie after steaks and potatoes will be just perfect."

"Steaks and potatoes, my favorite, how did you know?" They both laughed out loud. It was a good, relaxing laugh that put them both at ease. The dinner itself was not the uncomfortable part; it was the house being bugged and the police officers outside listening to every word that made the situation a little strange.

Riley broke the ice by telling him about Taylor's call. "It really freaked me out, him calling on the private line and all. I mean, Officer..." she stopped in mid sentence, it seemed odd to be calling her dinner date by his formal title.

He knew right away why she hesitated, "please call me Sean."

She relaxed a little more as they became more informal, "alright then, Sean. What was I saying?"

"He called on your private line..."

"Oh yeah, I never give that number to anyone. I can probably count how many people have that number on one hand. So you can understand why it's so weird."

"Riley, I think this whole situation is weird, but I'm willing to bet when we find Jeni and Kelsey and the identity of the woman driving the sport utility, the whole thing will fall into place and you'll have the answers you are looking for."

"You're probably right. All I keep thinking is if I didn't go to the bar with Kim that night, none of this would have happened."

"Well, let's put it this way, I know how old you are and you shouldn't have been in a bar to begin with, so if the bouncer had been doing his or her job and carded you, then, you're right, none of this would have happened."

Riley didn't know what to say. Sean seemed to sense that she was at a loss for words. He spoke softly, the sincerity in his voice was clear. "Riley, I didn't mean to say that. I mean, I meant to say that, but it didn't come out like it was supposed to. I know you and Kim were just out to have a good time and when I was your age, not too long ago, I did the same thing. I was just trying to make light of a stressful situation, I guess my attempt at levity wasn't as good as I thought it would be."

"Sean, you're right, I shouldn't have been there, but I don't deserve to be stalked by a crazy man and a woman who I've never met before, do I?"

"No, you don't and again, I apologize for by bad attempt at humor. Can you forgive me? I promise never to make a joke again."

She laughed, "I forgive you, but you can't keep that promise, I like to laugh, but the jokes have to be good ones."

"Fair enough. Now I'm starving and those steaks are beginning to smell really good out there on the grill. How about we eat?"

"Sounds good to me. If it's okay with you, I'll set up the table on the deck. I know you guys wired the house and I really don't feel like having the entire police department listening in on our dinner."

He didn't say a word, but when he picked up the potatoes and headed outside to serve the steaks, she understood he agreed with her. Dinner outside it would be. Once the ice was broken, the conversation flowed easily. Riley found him to be very interesting to talk with. He had only been a police officer for a few years and surprisingly enough, was only a couple of years older than she was. They talked about everything and anything. His hobbies, her hobbies, whatever came to mind, they just kept talking. He was very single, as was she, but he was a little leery of getting involved with her right now, he told her. He wanted to wait until everything was settled, for now he wanted to get to know her better. "I have an advantage, you know."

"Oh, and what might that be?" she chuckled.

"My job allows me to find out things that a regular guy wouldn't know."

"Like what?"

"Everything. I know everything there is to know about you, Riley Matthews."

"Oh, you do, do you? Well, since you know everything about me, I guess there's nothing more for you to learn, so what are you sticking around for?"

"That's an easy one. I like what I know and I'm sure there's much more to learn." He was smiling, staring at her as if he was about to kiss her. In the middle of the big mess that was going on around her, this guy managed to share an evening of fun with her, and now she was dreaming of him kissing her. He leaned over, his lips brushed hers, then he pulled away, "Riley, I can't. Not yet anyway." He looked at his watch, realizing it was after ten, he picked up the dishes and carried them into the house. "I really have to go. I enjoyed dinner, and I'd like to do it again, but let's get this other stuff out of the way first, okay?"

As much as she hated to see him go she knew he was right, she was entangled in a web of mystery and danger, one that he was in charge of solving and he couldn't concentrate on his job if she was distracting him, so she agreed. "I agree, let's find out what's going on and then we'll go from there."

He gave her a gentle hug and walked to the back door, leaving the way he came in.

Chapter 14

Riley closed and locked the door behind him. She heard the phone ringing, the private line again. Taylor was calling, her first thought as she reached over to answer it. She was wrong. She said hello, but heard nothing on the other end. Waiting a moment, she said hello again, this time she heard breathing on the other end, then whoever it was hung up and the dial tone rang in her ear.

"Did anyone trace that call?" She said out loud knowing full well that Officer Jackson was outside watching the house. No response. Then again, how could she respond? The wire in the house let them hear her, but did not let Riley hear them. She decided to call Sean's cell phone and ask him. It rang twice before he answered.

"Officer Patrick here."

"Sean, it's Riley. Did you guys get a trace on that last call? Whoever it was didn't say anything."

His voice sounded firm, "Riley, listen to me. I want you to stay in the house and keep the lights and alarm on. I'm going to send an officer up there to stay with you, but don't open the door to anyone until I call you and tell you the officer is knocking. I'll be back up there a little later. Understand?"

His tone frightened her, "Sean, what is it? What's wrong?"

"Riley, I can't talk now, just do as I say."'

"Fine." She hung up the phone a little annoyed as well as scared. What could have happened in the five minutes since he left here? It obviously was nothing good.

She began walking through the house, turning on all the lights as she went. The alarm had been set as soon as Sean had left, but she checked again to make certain. Once she had turned on all the lights, she had nothing else to do but sit and wait for the officer to arrive. Still unnerved by Sean's tone of voice, she decided it would be best to sit someplace close to the front of the house, if anything happened, she could get out through the front door quickly enough. She sat herself down in an easy chair in the front foyer, facing the windows. Outside she could see the blue police lights flashing, as she looked closely out the window she saw an ambulance arrive. Who was hurt? Riley was confused as to what could possibly be going on out there. A month ago her life was simple and normal, now it was a jumbled mess. "I just wish it would all end," she said out loud to herself. A moment later she heard a knock at the front door, at the same time her phone began to ring. Probably Sean she said to herself as she answered the phone. She was right, Sean was calling to let her know the officer was at the door. It was alright to open it and let him in, he also reminded her that it was very important that she listen to whatever the officer said to do.

"When will you be here?" she asked him.

"Riley, I don't know. Just let the officer in. I'll be there as soon as I can."

She opened the front door halfway, leaving the chain still intact. The man out front identified himself as Officer Marx and Riley recognized him from the police station the day before. She told him to wait a moment so she could undo the chain and let him in.

She closed the door and undid the chain, by the time she had reopened the door, Sean and another officer were standing next to Officer Marx. "Officer Marx, you take Officer Kent and patrol the house to make sure everything is the way it should be. I'll stay here with Ms. Matthews."

Officer Marx and Officer Kent nodded at Sean's orders, turned and began to walk the perimeter of the house. Sean looked at Riley with sadness in his eyes.

"Sean, please tell me what's going on?"

Closing the door, he took her by the hand and led her over to the couch. "Riley, there's been a terrible incident out front. Things are a little more out of control then we thought they were. "

"What happened?"

"Officer Jackson has been killed, her throat was slashed."

Riley gasped, "Oh, my gosh, by who?"

"We don't have a positive identification, but..."

"But what?"

He hesitated before he spoke, "Taylor is our main suspect, I'm sorry."

Tears filled Riley's eyes; there was no holding them back. The thought of Taylor killing another human being was beyond her imagination. She lost her temper and yelled at him, "What makes you think Taylor killed her? What about the woman in the black truck? She could have done it. I may not know Taylor all that well, but I don't think he's capable of slashing the throat of a police officer."

Sean let her vent her anger at him, then calmly told her the rest of the story. "The woman in the black truck has been identified as Maggie Benson, she's Jeni's sister. We're not sure why she's here..."

Riley cut him off, "Why don't you just ask her instead of letting her follow me around all day?"

Sean's firm response told her he did not like to be interrupted in mid-sentence. "Riley, don't tell me how to do my job. Ms. Benson will be questioned as soon as she regains consciousness. She had approached Officer Jackson's car, and most likely saw the stab wound, before she could leave the scene; someone hit her over the head and left her lying in the street. At first glance, she appeared to be dead and that's probably what saved her from really being killed. Whoever hit her thought they hit her hard enough to kill her. Fortunately for Ms. Benson and for us, they didn't. The doctor said she will regain consciousness, but he can't say when, so until she does, we're in limbo."

"In limbo?" Riley stared at him in disbelief. "What do you mean in limbo? Aren't you guys going to do something? You can't let a killer run loose. Officer Jackson is dead and someone tried to kill Maggie Benson, don't you think they might be trying to get to me? They were the two people standing between me and the world, so the killer is still out there and who knows when he'll try to get to me? There's got to be something you can do!"

"We're doing our best to keep you protected while we wait for Maggie Benson to be able to talk to us. She's the key to this puzzle and right now all we can do is sit and wait."

Sean was right, there was nothing else that could be done. They had officers patrolling her house and until something turned up, it was a just a waiting game. "Sean, can I go to the hospital and see Maggie Benson?"

He looked at her for a moment as if her request seemed unusual, but then his face relaxed, "maybe if you talk to her she'll wake up faster."

"Maybe. I'll get my coat and we can go."

Riley grabbed a coat from the hall closet and she and Sean walked out into the cold night air. It was well after midnight as they drove down the main road. The streetlights were off and the road was barely lit by the porch lights of the few houses along the way. It took them a few moments to reach the medical center; they parked in the section of the lot that was reserved for emergency vehicles and Sean told her to wait until he came around to get the door for her. He opened the door and did a quick scan of the parking lot as she got out.

"Take a look around, do you see any familiar cars?" He asked.

"You mean do I see Taylor's truck?"

"Yes, that's what I meant. Do you?"

She glanced quickly over the sea of cars and trucks, nothing stood out at her. "No, I don't see his truck or any familiar cars."

"Okay, then let's go inside." He put his hand on the small of her back as he guided her into the hospital entrance. Walking though the main doors, she saw an officer standing in front of an intensive care room. Sean approached him, hand extended, the officer greeted him with a firm handshake.

"Anything?"

"No, sorry Officer Patrick. The doctor just left, he said she was still out cold, gave her some medication and said he'd be back to check on her in thirty minutes or so. Said to have the nurse page him if there was anything she needed."

Sean thanked the officer and then opened the door to the room. Maggie Benson was laying in the bed, wires and tubes attaching her to three different machines. Riley stared for a minute, then prompted by Sean, walked over to the bed.

"Ms. Benson? Maggie? You don't know me, my name is Riley Matthews and I was a friend of Taylor's. At least I thought he was my friend. Things have been out of control lately and I know you were following him. What I don't know is why and I really need you to wake up and tell me what's going on." Riley was now on the verge of tears. The woman lying in the hospital bed could hold the answers to her questions. Riley desperately needed her to wake up.

Sean stood behind Riley, his hand on her back, gently letting her know that he was there for her. Riley was scared, this woman was badly bruised, what if someone wanted to do this to her? What if someone wanted to slash her throat the way Officer Jackson's had been slashed? A shudder ran through Riley. Sean apparently noticed her shaking as stepped closer to her, placing both hands on her shoulders, he leaned close to her and whispered in her ear, "it'll be alright, I promise."

That was all Riley needed to hear, she leaned back against him and closed her eyes. Breathing deeply she let the tears roll down her cheeks as he turned her around towards him. He wrapped his arms around her and held her tightly. Her tears flowed for what seemed to be an eternity, then she took a deep breath, wiped her eyes, stood up and turned to face him.

"Sean, thank you for being here. I know it's your job, but I really appreciate all the support you're giving me."

He didn't say a word, he placed his hands on her face and leaned over to kiss her. It started as a soft, gentle kiss, then became more passionate as she began to respond to him. When it was over, he looked her in the eyes and told her that he was not just doing his job, he wanted to be a part of her life and that's why he was here. "Do you understand?"

"Yes, Sean, I do."

They talked for a few more minutes, then she decided it would be best for him to get her some coffee while she stayed and talked with Maggie Benson. He left the room, telling the officer in front not to let anyone into the room while he was gone.

Once he left, Riley turned her attention back to Maggie Benson. She was feeling a little guilty for kissing Sean in her room, so she offered a quick apology to the sleeping woman, then continued, "Maggie, I hope it's okay to call you Maggie. Like I was saying, I met Taylor a short time ago and he seemed to be a really nice guy. Now the police are saying he killed an officer and knocked you out cold, so you can understand why they don't think he's such a nice guy anymore. I can't really blame them. After all, he's been spying on me for the past few days now and I must admit I find that a little creepy."

Riley didn't know if any of this was getting through to Maggie or not, but she remembered reading somewhere that by talking to unconscious people, it sometimes helped them to wake up sooner. She promised herself that she would keep talking until this woman opened her eyes and told her what she knew.

"Maggie listen, I know you must have a pretty bad headache from getting hit, but you really have to wake up. You're the key to this puzzle. I know you're Jeni's sister and if we could find Jeni, she'd be here, I know she would. The thing is Taylor told me Jeni was with your parents in Detroit, that she took Kelsey there until the divorce was final and things had simmered down.

The cops tried to find Jeni, but all they came up with is that the story was a lie. Your parents are dead, so therefore Jeni can't be in Detroit visiting them, can she? So where is she? And where is Kelsey? I think that is what you're trying to find out. I don't think Taylor ever knew your parents were dead. In fact I think maybe Jeni told him they were alive, why I don't know, but I think she did."

As Riley talked to Maggie, the story was beginning to make some sense. It was warped and bizarre, but the pieces were beginning to fall into place. She began to pace as she talked, her voice more animated with each sentence.

"I think Taylor thought your parents were alive and living in Detroit. I think you and Jeni pulled that off because you lived in Detroit and must have sent her letters pretending they were from your parents, Taylor probably never knew you existed; he just assumed Jeni was an only child. Then something happened to Jeni. She either left or maybe something even more tragic happened and when you didn't hear from her, you panicked. You called Taylor, pretending to be someone else, an old friend perhaps, and when you asked for Jeni, he told you she was in Detroit with Kelsey and her parents. Now, you knew the story was a fake, so your curiosity was peaked. You probably waited a few days, hoping that Jeni would call you when she got wherever she was going. Then when she didn't contact you, you decided to come here and investigate on your own."

Riley kept talking, the story making more sense as she went along.

"You went to the Squeaky Hinge because you knew Taylor's band played there; that's when you saw Taylor and me talking. You followed me home and then went back when I was out and asked Tony my name. Then you found the phone number and called the night Taylor and I met in the parking lot. Oh, my.."

"Riley, who are you talking to?" She had been so wrapped up in talking to Maggie, she hadn't heard Sean come back into the room.

"Sean. Maggie wasn't trying to hurt me, she was trying to protect me. I bet she's the voice on my answering machine. I think I figured out what's going on."

"Tell me."

They sat down and Riley rattled off the story she had pieced together by talking to Maggie's sleeping body. By the time she reached the end, Sean was as convinced of what was happening as she was.

"Riley, it makes some sense, but if you're right, Jeni and Kelsey are still missing and we have no idea where to begin to look for them."

"I realized that. The only person who can corroborate anything I just said is Maggie and she's out cold. Remember, the story is just something I made up, it makes sense to you and me, but we're outsiders, we could be totally off."

"A little off, but not by much, Riley."

Sean and Riley turned in disbelief and stared at the battered and bruised woman lying in the bed.

Riley spoke first, "Maggie? Can you hear me?"

Maggie managed a small smile, "yes, I can hear you perfectly. In fact I've heard everything you've said. Most of it was accurate. The details aren't that important right now. The important thing is that Jeni and Kelsey are missing."

"Ms. Benson, do you have any idea where they would have gone? Or do you think someone took them?" Sean had his notepad out and was ready to take notes when the doctors came in to examine Maggie.

Sean begged the doctors and nurses to let him ask just a few quick questions, but they were adamant in their orders, Riley and Sean were instructed to wait outside until the examination was finished. After the doctor gave the okay, then Sean could ask his questions.

They were escorted from the room and out to a small waiting area. They sat down on the fake leather couches and waited nervously for the doctor to come out and let them back in to question Maggie. It was after 3a.m. when the doctor emerged from Maggie's room. He dropped the chart off at the nurse's station and came over to talk with Sean and Riley. "Officer Patrick? Ms. Matthews?"

"Yes."

"I'm Dr. Anderson. Ms. Benson is sleeping comfortably right now. You can come back in the morning to talk with her."

Sean spoke up quickly. "Dr. Anderson, Ms. Benson is the key witness to a murder and may know where a missing woman and her child are. I cannot wait until the morning to talk with her. I'm sure you can understand that."

"Yes, officer I can understand that, but I must also keep the best interest of my patient as my main focus. Right now, Ms. Benson needs her rest. She has sustained an intense blow to the head, she is fortunate that she was not killed or maimed by the injury. She will recover to her full capacities within a few days, but for now it is most important that she gets as much rest as possible.

I have given her a sedative and she will sleep for the next four to six hours. You can sit here and wait or if you would like to take my advice, go home, get some rest, and come back to talk to her in the morning. Now if you will excuse me I have some other patients to attend to." He glanced at his buzzing pager and walked away from Riley and Sean, picking up a red hospital phone to answer the call.

Riley and Sean stared at each other for a brief moment. "Do you want to go back to your place? I can drop you off and then get you in the morning to talk to Maggie," he asked.

"Sean, I really don't want to go back to my house. I know it's crawling with cops and all, but I don't think I'll feel comfortable there." She sat back down on the couch in the corner. "I think I'll just stay here for the next few hours. I want to be here when she wakes up."

Sean sat down on the couch adjacent to hers, "I'll be right here with you then."

She smiled at him, he was going above and beyond the call of duty and he was most definitely watching out for her best interests. Reaching over to a bookshelf in the corner, she pulled out two pillows and two blankets, tossing him one of each and covering herself with the other. "See you in the morning."

"Sleep tight."

Riley closed her eyes and rolled over facing the back of the couch. She never would have been able to sleep in her house tonight. Not after a murder and an attempted murder had happened. She felt much safer sleeping in the hospital, especially since Sean was next to her. She didn't even have to turn around to know that he was not sleeping, but sitting up on the couch watching her sleep, protecting her from harm. With Sean watching over her, she could sleep soundly.

Chapter 15

"Riley, wake up."

She heard the voice over her and felt someone gently shaking her shoulder. It took her just a minute to remember where she was, the hospital. Then the previous night's events came back to her, the horrible scene at her house, the dead officer and Maggie. She sat straight up on the couch. Maggie! She must be awake by now. Riley rubbed her eyes and looked up at Sean standing over her with a cup of coffee and a can of orange juice.

"I didn't know which one you'd prefer." He reached out his hands offering her both the juice and the coffee.

"I'll take the coffee, thanks." It was lukewarm, hospital coffee, but it was better than nothing. She drank it down in three gulps. "Is Maggie awake?"

"Just woke up. The doctor is in with her now. He said as soon as he comes out, we can talk with her again."

They waited, anxiously watching for Dr. Anderson to exit Maggie's room. Riley wasn't sure what she was going to learn from talking to Maggie, but she knew that Maggie was the only lead they had. Dr. Anderson came out a few minutes later. Mimicking his steps from the night before, he brought the chart back to the nurse's station and walked over to Sean and Riley.

"Officer Patrick, Ms. Matthews, you can go in and see Ms. Benson now. Please keep it short and not too involved. The sedative has worn off and she's in a bit of discomfort, but she said she wants to talk with the two of you before I give her anything more to relieve the pain."

"We'll make it quick. Thank you doctor." Riley nodded in agreement with Sean's statement.

They walked over to Maggie's room. Sean exchanged greetings with the new officer on duty and they went in.

"Maggie?"

"Riley is that you? I asked them to let me talk with you last night, but the doctor said I needed to get my rest and he gave me a shot that knocked me out. I was so afraid you wouldn't be here this morning, or that something bad would have happened while I was asleep."

"Maggie, nothing more has happened, that's why we need your help. Do you remember who hit you?" Sean had prompted Riley on what to ask Maggie. He said sometimes women related to other women more easily and that it would be best if she talked with Maggie. She agreed.

"I didn't see him, but I think it was Taylor. I've been following him around for the past week or so and until yesterday I didn't think he knew he was being followed. Then last night, I saw him get out of the truck with something in his hand. I wasn't close enough to see what it was, but he went behind the bushes and then I saw him walk up to the car parked on the side of the road. He was hunched down, as if he was sneaking up on the driver. The next thing I saw was him reach in through the car window and the driver started moving around a lot. After that, he pulled his arms out of the window and walked away.

I got out of my truck and walked over to see if the driver was okay and when I looked into the car I saw a lot of blood and this woman with her head hanging down, she looked like a rag doll. I was in shock, I couldn't even scream. I started to run back to my truck to call for help and I remember turning around and then the next thing I remember is someone flashing a light in my eyes. After that, I remember hearing you talking to me last night. That's it. The woman in the car, she's dead right?"

She asked the question, but from the tone of her voice it was obvious she knew the answer already.

Riley told her "Yes, Officer Jackson is dead."

"Officer? She was a police officer?" Maggie looked over at Sean with wide eyes.

Sean responded to her, "Yes, she was a police officer."

"Why was she there?"

"We weren't sure what was going on, all we knew is that Riley was being followed by you. Then once we investigated, we found out that you were following Taylor and he was the one following Riley. We still didn't know who you were and we didn't want to scare you or Taylor off until we were able to catch you doing something wrong and we could bring you in. So we had set up a surveillance team and Officer Jackson was watching the house when she was killed."

"Well, I guess Taylor finally did something wrong, so you can bring him in, right?"

"We haven't been able to locate him," Sean said.

"What!" Riley was outraged. "You haven't arrested him? I thought that's what all the commotion was at my house. How could he have gotten away?"

Sean looked at Maggie and then at Riley. "Look ladies, Taylor seems to be cleverer than we had given him credit for. He has managed to stalk Riley for over a week without being detected and now he's the prime suspect in the murder of Officer Jackson and in Maggie's attempted murder. The guy knows we're looking for him. I know we're going to find him, and when we do, he's going to get the death penalty for killing a police officer in the line of duty. But we have to find him first, and Maggie, that's where you come in. You have to tell me everything you can about these past few weeks." Sean pulled a chair over and sat down at the side of her bed, he took out his notepad and pen, ready to take notes as she talked. "Start at the beginning, and don't stop until there's nothing left to tell."

Maggie looked at him, and then at Riley before beginning to speak, "here goes. Most of what Riley had said last night was true. Jeni is my sister and our parents are dead. They were killed in a fire a few years back. I was there when it happened. I was the only one to survive. The police did some investigating and they had always thought that Taylor had set the fire, to get Jeni alone in this world. Taylor was really warped, he told Jeni that he was all she ever needed and that she should cut off all contact with her parents, and with me.

Jeni loved him. She thought that if she loved him enough, she could convince him that she could have enough love for everyone and that he wouldn't suffer by her having a relationship with our parents and with me. A few years ago, Jeni got pregnant; she told Taylor that she wanted them to move to Detroit to be closer to her family. He went nuts on her, telling her that there was no way they would move to be near her family, that he was her family now and she should just get used to that. He even had their phone number changed and put a block on the phone preventing all long distance calls.

It was almost a month before she could get out of the house and convince a friend to let her use the phone to call us. The friend's husband had a big mouth and when the phone bill arrived he mentioned something to Taylor about it. Jeni told me that Taylor changed again after that; he became very loving towards her. She was now pregnant with Kelsey and he seemed to be relaxing a bit. He took the block off the phone and she called us regularly.

Then the fire happened. My parents' home burnt down in the middle of the night. I was supposed to take them to the airport in the morning to catch a flight to visit Jeni, so I had stayed over that night. Taylor didn't know I survived. When the police arrived and I learned that my parents had not survived, I was devastated. On top of that, the firemen told me that it was arson, someone had set the house on fire. I called Jeni while Taylor was out and told her what happened. I also convinced her not to tell Taylor about the fire or that our parents were dead. I wanted to see if he would slip up and say something, then they could arrest him. I was pretty sure he had set the fire." She stopped talking.

"Maggie, are you okay?"

"Yeah, it feels good to finally be able to talk to someone who doesn't think I'm crazy."

Riley had to ask, "Maggie, you said that Taylor and Jeni were married before Kelsey came along. What happened to her other children?"

Sean looked as surprised as Maggie was at the question, "What other children?"

Riley proceeded to tell them what Taylor had told her about Jeni following him from Detroit and leaving her first husband and children behind."

Maggie did not look surprised at the story. "Taylor has a way with words. He likes it when people think they are the ones with a problem, not him. He was always notorious for telling stories that were more fiction than fact."

"How long have you known him?"

"Jeni started dating Taylor many years ago. She was married before, but they never had the chance to have children. She had married her high school sweetheart, a guy by the name of Reid Paxton. Taylor was furious, he and Jeni had dated before she met Reid; but when she met Reid, that was it, she left Taylor and was going with Reid. They got married right after graduation, but Taylor never left them alone.

A few years later, Reid was killed in a hunting accident. Or so they say. He had been invited to go hunting with Taylor and a couple of his buddies. It was supposed to be a going away hunt for Taylor; he was going to move to Florida to go to scuba diving school. All I know is that four guys went out and only three came back. They all said it was an accident, somehow Reid got in front of the rifle, and since there was nothing to prove otherwise, it went down as a accidental shooting and Taylor stayed. He started courting Jeni again, and this time she was very vulnerable. They dated for several years and then finally got married about four years ago."

Riley was beginning to realize she couldn't believe anything Taylor had told her, it was all one big story. "I guess it's safe to say that Jeni didn't show up on Taylor's doorstep after he had left her in Detroit?

"My gosh, what did he tell you?" Maggie's blank facial expression told Riley was amazed at the intricate details of the stories about Taylor she had just told her.

"He told me that he was from Alabama and had moved to Detroit to play in a band. Then he met Jeni, who was married to one of the guys in the band and had a couple of kids. She started to flirt with him, he left Detroit to get away from her, then she showed up on his doorstep. She tricked him into letting her stay with him, got pregnant and therefore, he felt it was his obligation to marry her, so he did."

"The man is a bigger liar than I thought. The only part of the story that's the least bit true is the part about Taylor playing in a band. Other than that, the rest is bull."

Sean, who had been sitting quietly taking notes, jumped into the conversation. "Ladies, let's get back on track here. Maggie, do you have any idea where your sister and niece are?"

"No. Jeni called me a few weeks ago and said that Taylor was acting weird. He had said something to her about giving Kelsey up for adoption. He was a controlling man, and he didn't like the fact that Jeni spent a lot of time with Kelsey and couldn't devote a hundred percent of her attention to him. This was the straw that broke the camel's back, if you will. Jeni was fed up with Taylor controlling her and when he told her he wanted to give their child up for adoption... that's what put her over the edge.

She wanted to get a divorce, take Kelsey and move away from him. I told her she had to be very careful with what she said around him. She promised me she'd be careful and that she'd call me soon. That was the last time I heard from her. I called Jeni a week later. I got Taylor on the phone, I told him I was a friend from high school here on business, and really wanted to see Jeni. He was really friendly and told me how sorry he was but my timing was off and Jeni was in Detroit with Kelsey visiting her parents."

"Do you remember the exact date of that call?"

"No, but I'm sure it's on my phone bill. Why is that important?"

Riley wasn't sure what Sean was thinking, but his mind was obviously on the go.

He told her, "Maggie, that would be around the time frame that Jeni disappeared and if we can narrow it down to a few days we can check the airports and bus stations for a record of a ticket purchase. These days you can't fly with a child without going through an extensive identification check. If Jeni left town with Kelsey, she would have had to show id and once we find out where she was headed, we can find them."

Maggie gave him the phone number she had called Taylor from and the approximate date. Sean said he would have the station do a run down on the bill and come up with an exact date. He also took Taylor and Jeni's home phone number and the number Taylor had given Riley the night before. He figured the more information he could give them, the better chance they had of finding out where Jeni and Kelsey were. He told them to keep talking while he went out to call the station.

"He's very optimistic, but I'm afraid my sister is already dead."

Riley didn't know what to say. Maggie had been through a lot, but she had to think positively. "Maggie, think good thoughts. Jeni and Kelsey will come home safely. Until you see a body, you have to believe they are alive."

"Riley, I do think Kelsey is alive, it's Jeni that's dead."

"Why would you think Jeni's dead and Kelsey is alive?" Riley didn't want to have this conversation, but there seemed to be no way to avoid it.

"Like I was saying before, Taylor wanted to give Kelsey up for adoption. Jeni would never let her daughter be given away, so I'm pretty sure I know what happened. Taylor tried to get Jeni to give Kelsey up and Jeni fought him on it. He probably took Kelsey from her and then killed Jeni to stop her from going to the police. He may seem like a nice guy, but Taylor Martin is a devious, evil, self-serving man who will do whatever it takes to get what he wants. Even if it means killing his own wife."

Riley had nothing left to say. She felt the incredible desire to get out of the room and get fresh air. She quickly excused herself, assuring Maggie that the officer was outside and she'd be safe until she and Sean came back. She walked calmly to the door and walked out into the hallway, pulling the door closed behind her. She nodded at the officer on duty and then walked off towards the phone where Sean was standing. She gently tapped him on the shoulder as she continued past him into the waiting room. He came and sat down next to her a moment later.

"You okay? You're looking a little pale."

"The whole story is so warped. I just can't believe this is happening to me."

Sean put his arm around her shoulders, "Riley, we're getting closer. At least now we know what's going on. As long as we keep Taylor away from you, you'll be safe. It's Jeni and Kelsey who are in the most danger right now."

"Sean, Maggie thinks Jeni is dead and Taylor gave Kelsey away." As the words came out of her mouth, Riley remembered another movie of the week she had seen not too long ago, when the bad guys got caught through their bank accounts. "Sean, wait! I have an idea. Check the bank accounts. If Taylor is as warped as we think he is, he may not have given Kelsey away, he may have sold her. If he got money for her, then he would have had to deposit it somewhere. If we find the money, we can find the source of the money and then we find Kelsey!"

"Riley, you're a genius! I'm going to make a few calls, you stay with Maggie, I'll be back in a little while." He stood up and kissed her good-bye without realizing what he was doing. "Sorry, just seemed like the thing to do."

In the middle of the craziness, she laughed to herself as she watched him walk down the hallway towards the emergency entrance where he had parked his car the night before.

Riley stopped at the soda machine before going back in to sit with Maggie. She was putting the change into her pocket. She stopped and fumbled with the quarter. She looked around and saw a payphone in the corner of the waiting room. Without hesitation she picked up the phone and called Kim. On the third ring she answered. "Hello?"

"Kim, it's me Riley."

"Riley, where are you? The story is all over the paper about the cop who was killed in front of your house last night. What happened?"

Riley told Kim the abbreviated version of the story and then asked her to bring her some fresh clothes and some food. Kim said she'd find something and bring it over to the hospital as soon as she could. Riley hung up the phone and walked to the window drinking her soda.

It was a dark and rainy day outside; the weather seemed to be in sync with the events of the past few days. Everything had happened so quickly once she had gone to the police, maybe that is what triggered Taylor, or maybe it would have all happened even if she hadn't gone to the police. There was no way to know what would have been, she could only deal with "what is", and the "what is" that was happening was unnerving enough for everyone involved.

Chapter 16

Riley stood by the window for almost an hour before Kim arrived. Her hair matted to her face by the pounding rain outside, she still managed a smile as she walked through the hallway. "Riley, you look like hell."

The girls hugged tightly. Riley was never so glad to see Kim as she was then.

"Kim, it's been awful. People are being murdered and attacked all around me. Taylor is an animal. The woman in the bed in there, Maggie, is his sister-in-law. You would not believe the horrible things she has said about him and the worst part is that they all can be corroborated. The man has done such horrid things it's hard for me to think I ever saw any good in him. I feel like it's all my fault. If I hadn't talked with him and encouraged him, things would have been different. Kim, it's all my fault."

"Riley, it's not your fault. Things were going to happen whether or not you were involved. Taylor had an agenda and you just happened to be in the wrong place at the wrong time. That, my friend, is something I take the blame for. If I hadn't taken you to the Squeaky Hinge, you two never would have met and then this all would have been something we read about in the paper, not something we lived through." Riley looked at Kim, the sadness they both felt was overtaken by the strength they felt by supporting each other. "Kim, thank you for being here. It means a lot to me."

Kim put her arms around Riley and gave her a big hug, "I'm always going to be there for you, Riley. Now take this bag and go freshen up." Riley took the bag of clothing and went to the ladies room to change. She glanced back to see Kim pick up a magazine and begin to flip the pages while she waited. After freshening up, Riley returned at the same time Sean walked into the waiting area. Riley introduced them and then asked what Sean had been able to find.

"Well, you were right. Taylor had opened a new bank account in a fake name about six weeks ago. We traced it through his social security number. For a guy with the resources to get a fake id I was surprised he didn't get a new social as well."

"Guess it's pure luck he didn't."

"That's true, because if he had, we never would have caught it this easily. Anyway, the only account transaction was a deposit of fifty thousand dollars a few days before Maggie called him. We traced the check and came up with the name of an attorney that we're now trying to track down. Once we get a hold of him, we should have more answers."

Riley was glad to hear things were progressing, but she was almost afraid to ask her next question, "Sean, have your guys found any leads on where Taylor is?"

"No, we haven't been able to locate him yet. There's a video of him withdrawing five hundred dollars from the ATM yesterday and again today, but we haven't been able to find him since. At this point, we don't think he can get too far with a grand in his pocket, but then again, we don't know what his resources are." Just then Sean's pager went off. He excused himself and went to the nurse's station to use the phone.

"He's really cute, Riley."

"Kim, we're in the middle of a crisis here, now is not the time."

"Sure, whatever, he's still cute."

Riley blushed, "you're right, he is."

Sean returned quickly, "I'm going to head downtown, they brought in the attorney who gave Taylor the money, hopefully Mr. Greene will spill his guts easily and we can get things moving."

Riley froze. It was instinct when she heard his name, a chill automatically ran through her.

"Riley, you okay? You look like you've seen a ghost."

"Sean, did you say Mr. Greene? As in Kevin Greene?"

"Yes, do you know him?"

"Unfortunately, yes. The man is a money hungry beast who would do anything to make a dollar. He's the lowest form of scum there is."

"Well then it sounds like we may have the right man. He and Taylor would have gotten on just fine."

"Sean, take me with you. I want to be there when you question him."

"Riley, look I really wish I could, but you've been more involved in this case then you should have already. Normally, no one but the police would have been able to talk to the witnesses and you practically interrogated Maggie Benson single-handedly. I have to be more careful at the station house, I can't bring in a civilian to talk to suspects, it won't hold up in court. I'm sorry."

"I understand. Kim and I will stay here. Is it still okay for me to talk with Maggie?"

"You stay with Maggie and I promise to call you or come back as soon as I know more, okay?"

"Sure."

Again, he leaned over and kissed her gently on the cheek before he left. Kim smiled at her, "looks like you two are an item."

"I don't know what we are, he's a great guy, but right now with everything else that's going on around us, we haven't had time to really get to know each other if you know what I mean."

"Riley, he's the one, you know it as well as I do. When this whole thing blows over, he'll be knocking at your door."

"I hope so." She paused briefly then asked Kim if she wanted to come with her to talk with Maggie; Kim accepted the offer.

Chapter 17

Maggie was just waking up when they walked into the room. "Riley, is that you?"

"Yes Maggie, it's me. My friend Kim is with me."

They exchanged hellos and pulled up chairs to the side of the bed.

"Has anything more happened?" Maggie asked.

"Officer Patrick said they brought in an attorney that might have had something to do with giving Taylor a lot of money, but until they talk to him, we don't have any answers."

"How much money?"

"Fifty thousand dollars."

Maggie looked stunned. "Fifty thousand dollars, huh? I can't believe he would sell his own flesh and blood for fifty thousand dollars."

Kim looked confused, "sell his flesh and blood?"

Riley explained to Kim the possibility of Taylor selling Kelsey and tried to find a way to tactfully explain that Maggie thought Jeni was dead. Fortunately, Kim was able to pick up on Riley's vague explanation and didn't ask anything more. They talked more about the situation. Maggie divulged every tidbit she could about Taylor Martin. The more she talked, the more obvious it became to Riley that the man she met created a background that suited the needs of the situation. Riley was very angry with herself for being so gullible, but Kim and Maggie soothed her by reminding her how devious a man this was. She could never have known just how devious he was; therefore she was nothing more than a pawn in his game. She began to feel a little better at hearing that, but she said she would not feel completely better until Taylor was caught and Jeni and Kelsey were safe. No one said anything more. The phone rang, breaking the silence of the room. Riley answered it, figuring it would be Sean. Her guess was right.

"Riley, good news, he spilled his guts. Told us everything we wanted to know and even got some bonus information out of him. I'm on my way back over there; I have some questions for Maggie. Don't say anything though; I want to see her expression when I tell her about Kevin Greene."

Riley didn't understand why Sean would want to see Maggie's expression when he told her about Kevin, but she respected his wishes and agreed. Hanging up the phone, she told Maggie and Kim that Sean was on his way back, and he said everything was beginning to fall into place. Maggie asked her what she meant by that, but Riley, true to her word, just said she had no idea and was just repeating what Sean had said.

The nurse returned to Maggie's room and asked Kim and Riley to wait in the waiting area until she was done. They obliged and left the room. Once outside, Kim asked Riley what the rest of Sean's call was about. Riley took Kim to the corner of the waiting area and told her about Kevin Greene and Sean's request that she not say anything to Maggie.

"But why not?"

"I don't know, he said he wanted to see her expression. It's almost as if he thinks she was in on it or something."

"Very strange. I guess we'll know soon enough, he just pulled up, look."

Riley turned around to look out the window Kim had referred to, there was Sean and another officer walking through the parking lot. He was looking a little worn out, but then again, so was she. Neither one of them had been able to get a full night's sleep since this whole thing started. She had gone without any solid or restful sleep for over twenty-four hours now and he had gone without for longer than that. Once this was over, they could catch up on lost time, but for now they had a crime to solve.

The two officers walked in through the main doors, also with them was a court reporter, Sean headed over towards Kim and Riley as the other officer and the court reporter went into Maggie's room.

"Riley, anything new here?"

"Not at thing. What happened with Kevin Greene?"

"Well, why don't you and Kim follow me and listen in while I have a little chat with our patient."

They followed him into Maggie's room. She was sitting up in her bed when they walked in. "Officer Patrick, Riley said there was news, what is it?"

Sean's formality with Maggie took everyone by surprise. "Ms. Benson, I must advise you that before you answer any of my questions, you do have the right to remain silent and you have the right to an attorney if you so choose."

"What are you talking about? I don't need an attorney, I haven't done anything wrong."

"Very well, am I to understand that you are waiving your rights?"

"Yes."

"Ms. Benson, we have spoken with a gentleman by the name of Kevin Greene, do you know him?"

The color drained from Maggie's face at the mention of Kevin's name.

"Do you know him?"

"Yes."

"How do you know him?"

"I am married to his step-brother."

Riley gasped out loud. This was more than a slight turn of events, this was a full rotation. What was going on? "Ms. Benson, I'm going to ask you one simple question and I expect an honest answer. Do you know where your niece, Kelsey Martin is?"

All eyes in the room were focused on Maggie waiting for the answer.

She spoke in a voice almost too soft to hear, "yes."

Sean's voice boomed through the room, "where is she?"

"She's with my husband in Detroit. She's okay, she's safe, that's all that matters, isn't it?"

"That depends, Ms. Benson, do you know where your sister is?"

"No. That's why I came here, to find Jeni."

Riley was confused, why was Kelsey with Maggie's husband and what the heck was going on?

"Ms. Benson, do you know that purchasing a child is a criminal offense? You can go to jail for this."

Maggie spoke through the tears rolling down her face, "I never meant for this to happen. I was trying to help Jeni, I don't know how this all went so wrong."

Sean seemed to calm a little after seeing Maggie break down. "Maggie, I think it would be best for everyone if you told us what happened." She looked at him through tear-filled eyes as he handed her a tissue.

Maggie wiped her eyes and took a deep breath. "Jeni called me about two months ago and told me that Taylor was trying to put Kelsey up for adoption but in actuality he was trying to sell Kelsey. The reason I told you

about before was true, he didn't like Jeni having someone or something other than him to pay attention to. Taylor is a very sick man. Everything else I told you before was true. Taylor did set the fire that killed my parents, he accidentally admitted it to Jeni when he told her that he was going to give Kelsey up. He told her that she had two choices, she could give up Kelsey and they would get on with their life, just the two of them, or she could fight him on this and would have to live in fear of what might happen to her and Kelsey on any given day.

Jeni said she argued with him and he got really angry and yelled at her that if she didn't believe him, that was her problem, but to remember that her father didn't believe him either when he told him that something bad would happen if her parents didn't leave them alone. It was then that Jeni realized how sick Taylor was. He was a split personality, kind and loving one moment, then hostile and vicious the next. Jeni knew that she would have to outwit him in order to keep Kelsey alive. She loved that child and wanted to do whatever she could to keep her safe even if it meant sacrificing her own life." Maggie paused, the room silent as everyone listened to her every word, not knowing what she would say next.

"Maggie, please go on."

"Well, when Jeni called me and told me what was going on, she was really scared. She talked about running away with Kelsey, but she knew that if Taylor caught her, he'd kill her and take Kelsey without hesitation.

Like I had said before, Taylor never knew I survived the fire, he also never knew that I had gotten married and that my brother-in-law was an attorney here in Florida. My husband and I agreed that we needed to do something quick. We talked to Kevin and arranged for him to contact Taylor.

Taylor was so wrapped up in selling Kelsey that he didn't think twice when Kevin called him. Kevin told him he had a couple that were interested in adopting a toddler, and that we were willing to pay good money for a little girl. Taylor jumped at the chance and a meeting was arranged. Jeni never went to the meeting, just Taylor and Kelsey. Taylor told Kevin that his wife had died in childbirth and he was now dying of cancer and wanted to make sure his child would be well cared for after he was gone. He also said the only reason he would accept money for the adoption was because of the mounting medical bills.

Kevin said he was very convincing and that if he hadn't been in on it, he would have definitely believed every word Taylor told him. We gave Kevin seventy-five thousand dollars, he told us that seventy-five was the amount Taylor had insisted on, but I guess that wasn't entirely true, was it?"

"I'm sorry, but your brother-in-law managed to make himself a twenty-five thousand dollar profit on this deal."

"Figures, Kevin was never one to do a good deed for another, he was always into something for the money. Anyway, he met Taylor and got Kelsey from him. He put her on a plane with some friends of his who were traveling to Detroit. No one questioned it and we picked her up at the airport last month.

I thought by now I would have heard from Jeni, she never knew what Michael and I did to get Kelsey. I'm afraid she fought with Taylor and he killed her, so that is why I came here. Kelsey is safe and sound with my husband and a nanny in Detroit. Now, all I want to do is find my sister and catch Taylor, then I can go home happy."

"Ms. Benson, I cannot condone what you and your husband have done, but I can understand it. I just wish you were honest with us from the beginning. Why were you following Taylor?

"I was hoping he was holding Jeni somewhere and I thought if I followed him, he would lead me to her. I really don't know where she is, but I have this awful feeling that she's dead."

"Only Taylor Martin knows for sure. We're working on a few new leads right now and as soon as we know anything I'll let you know. For now, I need for you to call your husband and have him go to the Detroit police department with Kelsey, they need to see her in order for us to get positive identification and take her off the missing child bulletin." Sean took the phone from the nightstand and placed it onto the bed for Maggie to call Michael.

Sean left Maggie in her room with the second officer and he took Kim and Riley out to the hallway. "You two okay?"

Riley spoke first, "Sean, I can't believe this whole story. Just when I think it starts to make sense, something else happens and the whole thing shifts."

"I think it's all come together now. Taylor is the only one who can tell us what happened here, but at least we know that Kelsey is okay. Now if we can find Jeni..."

Kim spoke up next, "Sean, do you really think she's still alive? I mean, if Taylor took the money and sold Kelsey, don't you think Jeni would have turned up by now? I would think she would have called Maggie to let her know she was okay."

"I don't know. We have an all-points-bulletin out on Jeni Martin and so far nothing has turned up, no sightings at all. That's the strange part. Usually when someone disappears, there's a couple of sightings somewhere, but with this one, nothing. The only positive is that there's no body either. All the Jane Doe's at the morgue have been ruled out, so at this point we don't know what to expect." The officer in Maggie's room stuck his head into the hallway and motioned for them to come back in.

"I called Michael, he's going to take Kelsey to the station on 14th Street to be photographed and fingerprinted. Is that enough?"

Sean nodded, "Yes that will be fine."

"What happens now?"

Sean assured her that everything would be alright then told her that there would be a guard posted at her door for the rest of her stay in the hospital. After that, he couldn't say. "Once we find your sister or Taylor, we can go from there."

Maggie nodded that she understood and then said she was tired and wanted to rest. Sean, Riley, Kim and the court reporter all left so she could get some sleep.

Chapter 18

Sean asked Kim to take Riley back to her house and told her to stay there until they had more information. Riley didn't want to go, but he told her she had no choice. Her house was a crime scene with police barricades and a couple of armed officers guarding the house and there was nothing more she could do here at the hospital. His best advice was for her to go home with Kim and get some rest. After promising to call her as soon as he knew anything more, Sean walked them to the car and gently kissed Riley goodbye. She and Kim headed north while he headed south towards the police station.

They stopped at the local McDonalds before heading back to the house. Riley was craving French fries and a milkshake while Kim went for a cheeseburger and a soda. They talked about the weather and the movies, trying to avoid the reality that Taylor was still running loose on the streets and they were still in danger. Kim was about to pull out onto the service road when she spotted a tan sedan following them.

"Riley, did Sean say anything about sending a cop to follow us?"

Riley turned around in the seat, trying to get a clear look out the back window, "no, he didn't say anything about a tail."

"Then who's the guy in the tan sedan?"

"Don't know." She pulled out her cell phone and tried to call Sean. "Damn, the battery's dead. Can you see the guy?"

"Not clear enough to know who it is, or isn't for that matter."

Riley knew Kim was referring to Taylor. What if he was following them from the hospital? She had to think quickly. "Kim, drive back towards the police station, let's see what he does."

Kim pulled onto the service road and headed back towards the main road in the direction of the police station. The tan sedan still following them.

She ran through a red light and made a quick U-turn to get out onto the main road. That left the tan sedan sitting at the light. As soon as the light changed, he was back on their tail, catching up to them as they tried to get away. Finally, the tan sedan pulled up next to them on the passenger side, Riley glanced out the window uncertain of who she would see. The flashing lights on the dashboard and badge he was holding through the driver's window told her that the guy was a cop. She told Kim to pull over.

The officer was very understanding once she told him that Officer Patrick had not mentioned that someone would be following them and they apologized for any trouble they caused. The officer let them go with a warning, he understood that they were fearful of Taylor Martin, but he also advised them that they needed to watch out for the safety of others when they were driving. He said he would be following them back to Kim's house and would remain parked outside until he received further orders.

Kim drove back to her house cautiously, not wanting to cause any more commotion than had already been caused. They pulled in and watched as the officer parked across the street. Kim's parents were a little surprised to see Riley looking so haggardly, but once they explained what had happened, they were very understanding and supportive. Kim's father took his gun out of the cabinet and loaded it, "just to be on the safe side."

Riley was not about to argue, if for some strange reason, Taylor managed to find her here and tried to harm her, she felt better knowing that there was a loaded gun and a man who was an expert marksman here to protect her. Kim's mother made them some tea and Riley lay down on the couch to take a nap. It was easy for her to sleep in a house where there were people around; she felt there was safety in numbers.

Knowing what Taylor was capable of and what he would do next were two totally different things. She didn't know what his agenda was, but she knew he would not leave things unfinished. She was pretty sure he would try to contact her, when she didn't know, but she felt it would be soon.

The ringing of the phone woke her several hours later. Kim had put Riley's phone in her father's charger and it was now ringing incessantly. Riley rolled over and answered it in a groggy voice.

The man on the other end responded, "Riley? It's me." A shudder ran through her, it was Taylor on the phone.

Kim had come into the room when she heard the phone ringing; now she stood in the doorway looking at Riley's ghostly white face. She mouthed the words, "what is it?" Riley replied by writing Taylor's name on the scratch pad sitting on the table. Kim stared at Riley, seeming unsure of what to do. Riley tried to think clearly, wanting to do whatever she could to find out where he was without letting on that she knew what he had done.

"Taylor? Is that you?" She decided it was best to keep him talking while Kim went and got the cop sitting outside the house. She frantically motioned at Kim who was standing as if frozen, to go outside and get the cop. Her mind was racing, keep him talking, have to keep him talking, that's all that kept repeating through her mind.

"Yes, Riley, it's me."

"Where are you?"

"That's not important."

"Taylor, I really think we should talk, maybe I was too harsh before when I told you I had nothing to say to you." She looked up at the cop standing in the doorway listening to her conversation. He gave her the thumbs-up sign and motioned his hands for her to keep talking.

"Oh, now you've decided that maybe you were too harsh. You women are all alike, you think you can treat me one way and then you think I will turn around and forgive you when you realize how much you need me."

Her stomach turned. "Taylor, you're right, I'm just a woman, I don't know any better. That's why I need you so much, to guide me, to take care of me."

Silence. He didn't respond. Riley wasn't sure what to do next. The cop took a piece of paper and wrote "keep talking" in big letters. She waited another few seconds, then hesitantly said, "Taylor are you still there?"

"Yes, I'm here, I was deciding if I wanted to give you another chance or let you suffer with the choices you have already made."

"Please," she said in her best begging voice, thoughts of what this monster had done were fresh in her mind, she used them as motivation, she had to help catch him for Kelsey and Jeni's sake, "please don't desert me. I want to be there for you, to take care of you and only you."

"Ah, a smart woman, it's nice to hear you tell me what you really want. I am the man who can take care of you, I'm glad to hear that you finally realize that fact."

"Taylor, please, I want to be with you. Where are you? Where can we meet?" She was hoping that he would give himself away, telling her where he was would make things so easy, all she had to do was find out and that would lead the police right to him. He was too smart for that.

"Riley, listen to me. The police are looking for me. It's something really silly, I don't even know all the details, but a friend of mine was arrested and they asked him all these questions about me. Of course he wouldn't answer them, so they don't know where I am and I'm afraid if I tell you, they may question you as well, so for now I need you to do what I say and I will be able to come to you. Do you understand?"

By now, Sean had arrived on the scene with a crew of technicians. They hooked a wire onto her phone and were able to listen in through headphones. They heard him tell her to follow his directions; Sean nodded his head, as if to tell her to agree with whatever he said for her to do.

"Yes, Taylor, I understand. What I don't get is why the police would be looking for you, have you done something wrong?"

"Riley, shut-up, don't ask anymore questions or I'll hang up!"

His anger was apparent even through the phone. The look on Sean's face told her to cool it, keep calm and passive, not to challenge him. "I'm sorry. I didn't mean to question you. Please tell me what you want me to do and I'll do it."

"That's better. Now, I want you to head out to the beach and drive towards Atlantic Avenue. When you get there, turn onto Atlantic and keep driving until you get into town."

"Then what?" Riley knew the area he was talking about and if she drove too far into down, she'd end up in gang territory, not exactly a safe place for her to be.

"You just get there and I will find you."

"But how will I know if I've driven too far?"

"Just drive." That was the last thing she heard before the dial tone.

Sean looked at the technicians, "anything?"

"It looks like he was bouncing off a tower in Manalapan, but we can't pinpoint the location exactly."

"Well, how close can you get?"

"Within a five mile radius. He's somewhere in this area." The technician made a circle on a local map. Riley's house sat exactly in the middle of the circled area.

"You don't think he's at my house, do you? I mean, that would be crazy, to go back to the scene of the crime."

"He's not the most sane person now is he? I would not put it past him to be sitting right smack in the middle of the crime scene. Hell, if he could put his name on it and claim it as his own, he might just do that too!"

"So, what do we do now?" She asked.

"Well, first we put a wire on you and a tracking device on the car. Then we send you out there just like he said and we follow along until something happens." Sean seemed very secure in what he was saying. He wanted Riley to be calm, not to worry and most of all, not to act as if there was someone tailing her. She said she understood and would be okay, but something in her eyes told him she was more afraid at this very moment than she had been all along. Riley knew from the look in Sean's eyes that he wanted to reach out to her, to hug her and reassure her, but with a room full of people, it seemed as if he didn't want to cause any problems. At least that is what she told herself as he reached over and patted her on the back, telling her just to take her time and relax, that someone would be following her the whole way.

Riley wanted to be angry at Sean's lack of affection, but she convinced herself it had to do with the ten or so people standing in the room with them. She was nervous and scared, but if this is what needed to be done to get this psycho off the streets and to find Jeni, then so be it, she would do whatever it took.

They wired her up and fixed up Kim's car with the tracking device. Riley took her cell phone and checked the battery, it was a little low so one of the technicians replaced it with a new one. She said her farewells and drove off towards Atlantic Avenue, talking out loud a few times, making sure that the cops following her could hear everything she said. There was no way for them to acknowledge her other than to call her cell phone, so when it rang, it startled her

"Hello?"

"Riley, it's Sean, please stop talking out loud, we can hear you just fine. Stop worrying, we are right here and if anything happens, we'll be there right away."

"Sorry, just wanted to make sure you guys were there. I won't do it again." She hung up the cell phone as she turned onto Atlantic Avenue. At this time of day the traffic was heavier than usual and it was difficult to see through the flow of cars. She gave up trying to find Taylor or his truck, she kept driving, hoping that something would happen soon. Just as she came over the railroad tracks a car pulled up next to her and honked its horn. She looked over at the driver, a young kid with a baseball hat motioned for her to pull over. She turned into the gas station parking lot and locked her door. Then she cracked the window as he walked over to the car.

"You Riley?"

"Yes." She was not sure as to what was going on, but she had no choice but to play along.

He handed her a note through the window and walked away. He got into his car and drove off. Riley unfolded the note and began to read it out loud so the officers could hear.

"Riley, I tried to talk to you, I wanted you to meet me, but I had to make sure there was no one else with you. I am now satisfied that you are alone, so I can tell you where to go next. Turn the car around and drive back to your house. Before you get there, stop at the bank and take out as much money as the ATM will let you. We need a lot of money if we are going to get away from here. Now what?" she waited for the cell phone to ring, just as she finished refolding the note, the ringing began.

"Hello?"

"Riley, we heard everything you said. For now, just do as the note says. We're sending someone out to the house and over to your bank to try and intercept him. Hopefully he's relaxed enough that he will do something stupid like sit around and wait for you. When you get back to the house, drive slowly through the gate and whatever you do, don't pull around back. We have officers everywhere but there, we can't get a clean hiding place."

"I'll park in the driveway. When your guys get back to the house, make sure they get Sam off the property, I don't want anything to happen to him."

"Who's Sam?"

"He's the caretaker. He lives in the cottage out back."

"Riley, my men have been over the property at least a dozen times, there's no one else out there but them."

Riley was about to challenge Sean, but then hesitated as she remembered this was the time of year when Sam went to visit his wife's grave, to freshen the flowers and "talk" to her, as he once said. She was suddenly grateful for this trip, silently praying this mess would be long over by the time he returned.

"Don't worry Riley, he's not here. I'm sure wherever he is, he's fine."

"Yeah, you're probably right. I'm going to start the drive now. Are you guys following me in?"

"Yes. You won't see us and neither will anyone else who may be watching, but we'll be right behind you."

"Thanks." Riley put the car in drive and headed back towards her home. She pulled through the ATM at the bank and withdrew the limit of five hundred dollars. Then she drove back to her house. As she drove up the coast road she thought about how simple and boring her life was only a few weeks ago, now she didn't know if she would live to see another day. Maybe Taylor would kill her like he killed everyone else who got in the way. She told herself she was being ridiculous, that she needed to think positive and everything would work out fine.

She pulled through the gates slowly like Sean had instructed, and parked in the driveway. She got out of the car, leaving the engine running just in case. She looked around, not seeing anyone, she called out Taylor's name. "Taylor, are you here? It's me Riley, I have everything you asked for." No response. She tried again. "Taylor?" Then she heard movement behind her. She turned, expecting to find Taylor standing at the back edge of the driveway, her heart sank as she saw he was not alone. Sam had returned from his trip and now Taylor was holding a gun to Sam's head.

"Look here Riley, I found a friend of yours putting some suitcases in that car over there." He swung the gun towards the back side of the property where Sam lived.

"Taylor, he lives there. It's okay, he doesn't mean any harm."

"Oh, I know he won't hurt us. It's just that he's seen me and you together and since he's the only one who knows that we're running away together, he's a bit of a problem, you do understand, don't you?"

Sweat ran down her face. She had to think fast, otherwise Taylor was going to kill Sam and she couldn't let that happen. "Taylor, listen to me. You don't want to hurt him. He takes care of the house and if he's not here then I have to go and find someone else to be here and that's really hard to do these days. If he stays here, I can go away with you, but if he can't be here to take care of things, I have to stay, and you can't stay with me. You'd be all alone with no one to take care of you. Is that what you want?"

Taylor adjusted his fingers around the barrel of the gun, they were turning white with the firmness of his grip.

"You said you had what I asked for, let me see it."

Riley held out the five hundred dollars she had gotten from the teller machine for him to see. "See, it's all here. I can get more tomorrow and the next day too. We'll never have to want for anything again."

He seemed a little more relaxed now that he had seen some money, but he still didn't let go of Sam or the gun he held to the back of his head. "How much is there?"

"There's five hundred here and like I said, I can get more each day."

He yelled at her, "No! Not how much is there, how much is there in the bank?" Riley was taken aback; she didn't know how to answer that question without causing more trouble. "I don't know. There's enough though."

"Don't lie to me Riley! Kevin Greene said that you were loaded. Millions of dollars at your fingertips, rich beyond belief. Is that true?" He was acting like a madman now.

She was even more surprised. What would Kevin Greene be doing talking to Taylor about her money? "Taylor, how do you know Kevin Greene?"

Taylor seemed proud that he had unnerved her. "Kevin and I go way back. When I moved here I needed a little legal help, so he managed to help me out of a scrape while I helped him to make some money. You could say one hand washes the other."

"What did he tell you about me?"

"Oh, he liked you. Said you were a pretty rich girl whose parents died in a plane crash. Left you millions of dollars and you hadn't spent a dime since they died. What a shame. I personally thought you and I could hit it off and once we were married, I could help you spend some of that money."

"Are you telling me that our meeting was not a coincidence?"

"Well, that's the funny thing, here I was trying to figure out a way for Kevin to introduce us in a nonchalant manner and you come walking right into my life. I couldn't have planned it more perfectly. I called Kevin the night after we met and he told me about your boyfriend. I knew I needed to move fast to get you two apart, and again you made that easy too. Everything just fell into place, can't you see, things happen for a reason. We were brought together because it was meant to be."

Riley felt her stomach heave; she wasn't sure how much more she could take without throwing up all over him. "Taylor, look, if this is meant to be then you should let Sam go and we can go off together just like you want." She wasn't sure what she was saying anymore, only that Sam was important to her and she was going to do whatever it took to make sure he didn't get hurt.

"Nice try, but I think we'll keep Mr. Sam around for a little while longer." He waved the gun in the air, motioning towards the house. "Let's go inside, it's getting a little too visible out here."

Riley had hoped he hadn't noticed the police around the house, but apparently he did. She wasn't sure what would happen once they were all inside, but at this point she had no choice in the matter. She used the remote to open the garage door, disarming the alarm as they went in. As they went through the door, Taylor directed them towards the kitchen. Again Riley was taken aback by his familiarity with her and her home. "Taylor, how long have you been watching me?" She was scared for both herself and for Sam, so she figured that the best thing to do was keep him talking that way the situation could become a little less tense. It seemed to work as she asked the questions he rambled on about how easy everything was.

"Oh, Riley, I've been watching you for weeks now, you're so beautiful I couldn't resist when Kevin told me about you. The perfect woman, yet all alone in this world, in need of a strong man to take care of you. And with so much money, it's amazing how much one could accomplish with that much money at his fingertips. All I wanted was to take care of you, to treat you like a princess and of course, myself as the king of the castle. We would be so perfect together, but then again there were things that had to be taken care of before we could have our perfect life."

Riley glanced at Sam, he looked pale and exhausted sitting in the chair next to Taylor. She prayed nothing would happen to him, she would never forgive herself if Taylor hurt him. The cops were still outside and thanks to the wire she was wearing, they could hear every word that was said. Now there was nothing left to do except to keep him talking while the police looked for the opening they needed to take him down.

"Taylor, you keep saying everything would have been perfect, but what about your wife and daughter, weren't they in the way?" As soon as the words were out of her mouth, she almost regretted mentioning Jeni and Kelsey, but she knew they were the key to this situation and if Jeni was ever going to be found, they needed as much information as possible.

"Riley, you are a smart girl." He was pacing now, sweat beginning to appear on his forehead. He was still clutching the gun in his hand, his fingers turning white with the lack of blood flow allowed by the tightness of his grip. "They were in the way, that's all they ever were. Jeni was a problem from the start, she just wouldn't listen to me when I told her what to do! Then she has the nerve to get pregnant, I told her I never wanted any kids, but there she went again, not listening to me, trying to live her own life, the nerve of that woman! I showed her who's boss, now she listens to me!"

He was talking about Jeni in the present tense, this was a good sign. Maybe she was still alive. "Taylor, where is Jeni now?" She prayed that he was agitated enough to answer her without thinking, to give her an honest answer so that the police could get to her quickly. She wasn't so lucky though.

"Jeni was always so self-centered, never concerned with taking care of me. Then she had that kid and everything changed even more. Now, not only did she not take care of me, we also had a screaming brat to contend with." His pacing was making her nervous, the gun still in his hand; he was becoming more agitated with each step. She tried to get a closer look at Sam as Taylor paced around the kitchen, but her eyes were so tired, all she could make out was the paleness of his face and his trembling hands. Time was not on their side, if she didn't get Sam out of the house and to the hospital soon he might not make it. The strain of the situation was wearing on the old man and it was becoming apparent by his appearance.

She decided to take the direct approach, "Taylor, tell me, where is Jeni?"

He stopped pacing. Turning to face her, his eyes meeting hers, "where is Jeni?" He let out a sick laugh, half laugh, half choke. "You want to know where Jeni is? I suppose you want to know where that little brat is too?"

Riley saw her opening and took it, "no, I'm not interested in knowing where Kelsey is, I know that already. I just want to know where Jeni is."

Her response took him by surprise. "What do you mean, you know where Kelsey is?"

Now it was her turn to laugh. She decided to try and bargain with him. "Taylor, I know what you've done. You sold your own child, but what you don't know is that you sold her to someone I know. She's happy and healthy living with her new parents. If you want to talk more about her, you'll have to offer me a deal; otherwise, I have nothing else to say about her."

He hesitated briefly, loosening and tightening his grip on the gun barrel. "What kind of deal?"

"Let Sam go. He's an old man, look at him, he's obviously sick and in need of a doctor. Let him walk out of here and I'll stay and talk with you about anything you want to know."

He considered her proposition for a moment, then shook his head. "I can't let him go, he'll go right to the police and then they'll come here. No, I have another idea, if you want him out of his misery; I'll take care of that right now." He raised the gun to Sam's head, but before he could pull the trigger, she called out to him.

"Taylor, No! The police are already here and if you kill Sam, they'll come charging in here faster than you can imagine. Then it will all be over and you and I will never have the chance to live happily ever after."

His blank stare told her he did not know the police were outside. He pulled back the curtains and saw the swat team in position around the house. Several police cruisers were in the driveway, prepared to take him down with force if necessary. Once he pulled back the curtains, the police flashed a light into the window, preventing him from seeing the officers and therefore preventing him from shooting at them. He let the curtains go, falling back into place over the window.

Turning to her, "how did the police get here?" He was yelling louder than she had ever heard. He grabbed her by the arms and shook her, "tell me, how they got here?"

"They were here before I got here. Taylor, everyone knows what you've done. There's nothing else you can do but give yourself up. Tell them where Jeni is and maybe they'll go easy on you." She hoped and prayed that he would listen to reason. There was no telling what he would do now that he knew the police were outside.

He began rubbing his temples, the gun still tightly gripped in his hand. He stared at the floor as he resumed his pacing.

"I can't believe you would do this to me! All I ever wanted to do was love you and you are making that so hard. I have to think, just be quiet!" The glare in his eyes told her that she should keep as quiet as a mouse if she wanted to get out of this alive. She and Sam sat there for what seemed an eternity, while Taylor paced the floor rubbing his temple and mumbling to himself.

About ten minutes later the phone rang, breaking the silence of the room. He stared at it as if it was a foreign object. Riley knew by the ringing that it was the police, she watched and waited to see if he would answer it. After the fifteenth ring the phone stopped.

Then it was Sean's voice over a bullhorn that roared through the house. "Taylor Martin, I know you're in there, I want to talk to you. I'm going to ring the phone again, this time I want you to answer it."

As if on cue, the phone rang again, this time he motioned towards Riley with the gun, "get it."

She reached over to answer the phone, never taking her eyes off of him. It was on the fifth ring by the time she picked up, "hello?"

Sean was not expecting to hear her voice, "Riley? Riley is that you?"

"Yes, this is Riley." She wanted to remain calm, if Taylor knew that she was dating one of the cops outside he might not be as friendly as she needed him to be.

"Are you alright?"

"Yes, Officer we're all fine." Taylor grabbed the phone from her hand. "Listen here Officer, get your guys out of here or there's going to be a lot of trouble!"

"Now Taylor, you don't mean that. I want to settle this thing just as much as you do. So why don't you let Riley and Sam go and I'll come in there so we can talk?"

Although Riley couldn't hear what Sean was saying, she figured it had something to do with Taylor giving himself up. Taylor seemed to be thinking about what Sean was saying. "Look, I'll let the old man go, but no one is coming in here yet. I have some things to talk to Riley about. You understand me?"

Sean must have agreed to the terms because Taylor grabbed Sam by the arm and gave him a shove towards the door, "get out old man!"

Sam looked at Riley as he walked towards the open door.

"Sam, it's okay, go, I'll be fine." She wasn't sure what was going to happen next, but the situation was out of her hands, she was just along for the ride.

Taylor slammed the door closed behind Sam, turning to look at her. She saw an evil in his eyes she had never seen in anyone before. Up until that moment nothing had been real to her, she had been living in a wild nightmare, but now the nightmare was reality and her life was at stake.

"Riley, we have to talk. Please come sit with me." He patted the chair next to where he was standing. Her feet moved as if they had a mind of their own. Slowly she walked towards him, her fear mounting as she grew nearer. She sat down without looking at him, staring at the countertop and hoping he would just leave her alone. No such luck. He began stroking her hair as he stood behind her. She could feel his hot breathe on her neck, smelling her hair; she tried not to cringe with his touch.

Finally he spoke, "Riley, you know what I've done for you, don't you?"

She kept her eyes focused on the countertop, slowly she nodded her head. Her strength was draining slowly, she was all alone in the house with him and she lacked the energy to challenge him.

He was not satisfied with her answer, grabbing her by the hair, he yelled, "answer me!"

"Yes" she managed in a meek voice, "I know what you did for me."

"Tell me." He was very nonchalant, as if he wanted her to retell the story of his horrible actions, like a child wanting to hear his favorite story over and over again.

She relented. "You sold your daughter and killed several people so that we could be together." Her stomach turned.

"You don't sound pleased, Riley. You should be flattered at what I have done so we can be together. Why aren't you flattered?" His voice echoed through the kitchen as he swung his arm around knocking the porcelain canisters off the counter and smashing onto the floor. Riley began to shake as the tears rolled down her face. "Answer me!"

She tried to talk, her voice reflecting her fear, "I, I am flattered. It's just that so many people got hurt because of me and I feel really bad about that. No one had to die, especially Jeni. You left a little girl without her mother and I know what that's like, I lost my mother too."

For a moment she thought maybe she should not have said anything about Jeni being dead, after all there was no proof she was dead and what if that put him over the edge? On second thought, there was not much more she could lose so why not risk it all? He was standing a few inches away, his eyes cold as he glared at her, "So, you think I killed Jeni? What else have they told you about me?"

Riley regained her composure, he seemed to calm down a little and this might be her only chance to have a rational conversation with him, she had to be calm. "I know you sold Kelsey, you used the attorney to work a deal, but what you didn't know is that the person buying Kelsey was..."

"Maggie Benson."

His words stopped her in mid sentence. "What? You knew?"

"Yes, I knew. That's the reason I was okay with it. Yes, I did a lot of things wrong, but I never wanted to hurt Kelsey or Jeni. I love them both so much, but it was wrong. I knew you and I were supposed to be together and for that to happen, things had to change."

Her head was starting to throb, she thought she knew what was going on, but apparently she was wrong, or at least not entirely right. "Taylor, you sold Kelsey, right?"

"Yes, Kevin said he had a couple that wanted her. I knew if she had a good home then I wouldn't have to worry about her, contrary to what people may have said, I loved her, I just didn't want her around. Okay, so that may not sound so great coming from a father, but at least I didn't hurt her, I made sure she went to someone who would take care of her and love her as much as I did."

He was right, that didn't sound normal, but then again, Taylor was far from normal. "So you gave Kelsey to Kevin and he gave her to Maggie, but what happened to Jeni? Everyone thinks you killed her. Where is she?"

Time was passing quickly and Taylor was becoming more and more relaxed as he spoke about what had happened, as if she had hit the right button and it was all coming out now, this was his release, he was finally coming to terms with what he had done. Tears formed in his eyes as he began to speak, "Jeni is dead. I don't know where her body is. You'll have to ask Kevin Greene about that."

"Why Kevin Greene?"

"He buried her after he killed her."

The shock almost overwhelmed her, "Kevin killed Jeni?" In the back of her mind she remembered that she was wired, the police could hear everything that was being said and she wanted to make sure they heard her loud and clear, "Taylor, did you just say that Kevin Greene killed Jeni?" She could see the officers running around outside through the kitchen window, she was certain someone had given the order to arrest Kevin Greene. She turned back to Taylor.

"Yes that's what I said." It was at that moment his strength broke and the tears came. "Kevin promised me no one would get hurt, but then Jeni showed up and began ranting and raving about how Kelsey was her daughter and no one could take her away from her.

Kevin told me to shut her up, he was afraid that other people might hear her screaming, so I tried to grab her and cover her mouth. That didn't work; she just squirmed around more and broke through my grip. Then Kevin handed Kelsey to me and grabbed Jeni by the shoulders really hard. He told her to shut up or she would get hurt. She just screamed louder and Kevin shoved her against the brick wall. All I heard was a thud as she fell. I thought she was dead, but then she began moaning. Kevin took Kelsey and gave her to one of his thugs, handed me my money and told me to get out of there. He said he would take care of things.

I was in shock; I didn't know what else to do, so I took the money and ran. Once I got out of the building I threw up, I was so scared thinking about what was going to happen next I couldn't focus. I found the nearest bar and started drinking. The next thing I knew the sun was coming up and I was lying in a hotel room with some girl whose name I didn't even know. I haven't seen Kevin since that night."

The situation at hand seemed to have calmed with his confession, so Riley was thinking about asking more questions, but she didn't know where to begin. She decided to go with her gut instinct and see what happened.

"Taylor, did you kill the police officer who was in front of my house?"

He looked at her as if wanting the answer to be different than the reality, "Yes, I did. I have no excuse, it just happened."

He sat quietly, waiting for her to ask her next question. It did not take long for her to know what she was going to ask about. "Did you kill Jeni's parents?"

"You mean, did I burn the house down? The answer is no. If you mean did I hire someone to burn the house down, then the answer is yes."

His candor was amazing her. At this point, he probably realized there was nothing more he could do, the situation was going to end with his capture, so why not tell all and satisfy her curiosity. "What about Reid Paxton?"

"That one I took great pleasure in. The guy was a bastard and deserved to die. He beat Jeni all the time and no one said a word about it. A couple of the guys and I took him hunting and turned him into the hunted. Trust me, he died a long and painful death. Next question."

To him this was becoming a game show with Riley as the host asking the questions and Taylor as the contestant with all the right answers. She didn't have much left to ask about. "What's going to happen now?"

He took a deep breathe and lowered the gun he had been holding so tightly in his hand. He leaned over to her and gently kissed her on the cheek. Looking her straight in the eyes, he smiled slightly, "Riley, you get out of here. I need some time to think about what I have done. I know what the consequences will be so if you don't mind, I'd like to take these last few minutes to enjoy what freedom I have left."

She stood up slowly, still a little dazed by what had just taken place. Her instinct was to reach out to him, but the fullness in her stomach reminding her how much of a monster he really was, prevented her from doing so. She walked to the door, stopping briefly, she turned back to him, "what should I tell them?"

He knew she was referring to the officers outside. "There's nothing left to tell, they heard it all through the wire you're wearing. For now, I'd just like a few moments alone."

She turned around and walked out the door, collapsing into Sean's arms as she came out the garage door. He stroked her hair and held her tightly as she breathed the night air deeply into her lungs. Through her sobs she asked about Kevin Greene.

"We got him," he told her, "it's all over."

"But Taylor is still inside."

"Not for long. " As the words came out of his mouth a single gunshot echoed through the dark night. Riley stood straight up and looked at Sean. He was staring at the house in disbelief.

Her body began to shake as she heard the voice of the officers inside crackle over the radio, "get a medic in here, suspect down, self-inflicted wound to the head, get someone in here, now!"

The surprise was not as great as she thought it should have been. Replaying their conversation in her head, she knew he wasn't coming out alive. He wanted to enjoy his last few moments of freedom before he took his own life. His story had been told and now he knew he could leave this world without leaving any questions unanswered. She watched as the medics rolled his body out in a body bag and put him into an ambulance. They pulled away without the lights or siren, it was too late now, there were no more chances left for Taylor Martin. She shuddered as the cool ocean air blew through her. Sean held her as they walked to his car, "Come on, let me get you out of here."

Without a word she climbed into the car and they drove off in the direction opposite the ambulance.

Epilogue

The police arrested Kevin Greene that night and he spent the next seven months awaiting trial in the county jail. Eventually, he was tried, convicted and sentenced to fifteen years in jail for the murder of Jeni Martin and for his role in the sale of Kelsey Martin. The body of Jeni Martin was never recovered. Kevin Greene admitted to burying her in a shallow grave on a nearby construction site that has since been cemented over.

Kelsey Martin was legally adopted by Maggie and Michael Benson and is now a happy healthy twelve-year-old living in Michigan.

Tony stayed in touch after the incident occurred, but eventually he and Riley drifted apart when he realized there was no chance of them getting back together. He now lives in California and is working for a cruise line as a bartender and blackjack dealer.

Sam recovered from his ordeal and continued to live in the cottage in back of the house; he died quietly in his sleep two years after the incident.

Today, Riley is happily married to Detective Sean Patrick Murphy. She juggles being a mom and spending time with their four-year-old twins, Samantha and Jeni, with assisting clients as a private investigator.

Kim is a frequent visitor to the Matthews-Murphy Estate, godmother to the children and Riley's partner when it comes to surveillance work.

The memory of Taylor Martin still lingers, but for Riley, the nightmares are fading with time. His body was sent back to Michigan and is buried near the Benson home where he was raised. As time went by, everyone went on with their lives, trying to rebuild after the wreckage that was caused by Taylor Martin. It has taken many years, but the memory of that horrible night has finally begun to fade and as each new day dawns, the beauty of life is renewed in the minds of those who survived the wrath of a madman.

An excerpt from the next Riley Matthews Mystery:

"There is no connection and I really wish you would stop saying that there was!" He shouted at her.

Riley hollered back, "There is, I know it and if you are just too stubborn to see it yet, that's your issue, not mine!" She turned to storm out of the room, her arm hitting the table and the stacks of photos falling to the floor. Leaning down to pick them up, something caught her attention. From the photo of the rec room a book seemed to stand out from the others on the shelf, as if it did not belong there. It was taller than the others, light in color with a unique emblem on the spine. "Ken, give me your magnifying glass!" She said out loud, reaching her hand out.

"What are you looking at?" Ken asked placing his magnifying glass into her hand and moving to stand over her shoulder.

"This" she said holding the glass so he could what she was pointing to in the photo. "See that book? I'd swear I've seen something like it before. Hang on a sec." Riley reached over to her bag and from the back compartment she pulled a red file marked "private" and began flipping through the photos inside. She found what she was looking for and handed the magnifying glass back to Ken along with the second photo, "here, look at this. What do you see?"

"What's that?" Ken asked as he glanced at the two pictures.

Riley pointed to the book on the shelf in the first photo and to a similar book laying on a bedside table in the photo she had pulled out her red folder. "Do you see what I see?"

As Ken leaned over and looked at the pictures, Riley flipped through her folder again, pulling out another photo and placing it next to the two already on the table. Ken looked back and forth over the three photos and then looked up at Riley. "Where did these come from?"

"The first one is your crime scene; the other two are from the other cases I was talking about. Do you believe me now when I say they are all related?"

"I don't know Riley, it's just a book, could be that the victims all had similar tastes in literature." He said flatly. Riley stared in disbelief as Ken then started to walk away.

"Hey, where are you going? We're not done here!" She yelled at his back.

"We'll never know until we find out what that book is. I'm heading back to the scene, are you coming or not?" He replied without turning around.

Riley grabbed her bag and the photos, tossing them all inside as she tried to catch up with Ken, who showed no signs of slowing down to wait for her. She jumped into the elevator just a split second before the doors began to close. "So I guess this means you're coming?" He chuckled. The doors closed as he pressed the button marked "G" and with a whirring noise the elevator began descending three floors below to the parking garage.

About the author:

Caryn Gottlieb FitzGerald has been sharing her love of the written word for over 25 years. She currently resides in Texas with her family.

For previews and more information please visit: www.CarynFitzGerald.com.

www.ingramcontent.com/pod-product-compliance
Lightning Source LLC
Chambersburg PA
CBHW052147170626
46812CB00004B/1627